Various Antidotes

VARIOUS ANTIDOTES

stories

JOANNA SCOTT

PICADOR

HENRY HOLT AND COMPANY

NEW YORK

www.picadorusa.com

Picador® is a U.S. registered trademark and is used by Henry Holt and Company under license from Pan Books Limited.

For information on Picador Reading Group Guides, as well as ordering, please contact the Trade Marketing department at St. Martin's Press.
Phone: 1-800-221-7945 extension 763
Fax: 212-677-7456
E-mail: trademarketing@stmartins.com

Designed by Kate Nichols

Library of Congress Cataloging-in-Publication Data

Scott, Joanna.
    Various antidotes: stories / by Joanna Scott.
        p. cm.
    ISBN 0-312-42387-X
    EAN 978-0312-42387-2
    Contents: Concerning mold upon the skin, etc.—Bees bees bees—Nowhere—The marvelous sauce—Chloroform jags—Dorothea Dix—X number of possibilities—Convicta et combusta—You must relax!—A borderline case—Tumbling.
    I. Title.

PS3569.C636V37 1993
813'.54—dc20

                                                                    93-18408
                                                                    CIP

First published in the United States by Henry Holt and Company

First Picador Edition: April 2005

10 9 8 7 6 5 4 3 2 1

To Kathryn

Contents

ACKNOWLEDGMENTS

These stories previously appeared in magazines: "Concerning Mold Upon the Skin, Etc.," *Antaeus*; "Bees Bees Bees," *The Yale Review*; "Nowhere," *Conjunctions*; "Dorothea Dix: Samaritan," *Epoch*; "X Number of Possibilities," *The Iowa Review*; "Convicta et Combusta," *Conjunctions*; "You Must Relax!" *The Paris Review*; "A Borderline Case," *The Paris Review*; "The Marvelous Sauce"—previously published by French Broad Press, Asheville, North Carolina, with an introduction by Paul West. I am grateful to the John D. and Catherine T. MacArthur Foundation for its support.

VARIOUS ANTIDOTES

CONCERNING MOLD
UPON THE SKIN,
ETC.

He was a man distracted by his ignorance, acutely aware of the limits of his knowledge and therefore superior, in his own opinion, to his ignorant and complacent neighbors. He wanted to know what he didn't know and since his youth had devoted himself to the effort of knowing more. Not Faustian ambition but fresh wonder kept him awake at night, caused him to break out in a cold sweat when he held up a finished lens to a candle flame, displaced all other appetites. And even though his neglected wife took to entertaining suitors in her own bedroom and his horns were visible to everyone, he didn't care. He cared only about what was unknown, believed that what the human eye could see or the ideas that the mind could conceive constituted a mere fraction of the world. Most of his contemporaries were satisfied with the dual concepts of substance and spirit. But even as a child he had sensed that the world of substances did not end with man's perception of it. Just as the sky disappeared into the invisible heavens, the material world disappeared into its invisible parts and so could never be examined in its entirety.

The obscurity of minutia thrilled and maddened him—literally drove him mad. When he was a young man of twenty-six he built a laboratory in the back of his dry-goods shop, at first simply a room where he could be alone with his experiments but eventually the room in which he ate, drank, and slept. On the day he dragged his bedding into the laboratory, his wife stopped pleading with him and offered herself to an eager gallant. Too distracted by love and lust ever to give her husband a second thought again, she left it to her eldest daughter Marie to carry in her father's meals, which he hardly touched, and later in his life, to bring him his mail, which he devoured with insane, carnivorous impatience.

Born in 1632, he was a citizen of Delft, a linen-draper by profession as well as an official of the Delft City Council. And it must be said on his behalf that for many years he continued dutifully to measure and cut and sell his bolts of cloth, despite his consuming passion. Every day but Sunday he tended the shop, and he spent three evenings out of the week examining the newest weights and measures in the City Hall. He worked at these jobs that he detested with stoical persistence in order to support his family so that they would leave him alone.

Alone. How he loved the solitude of winter nights, his laboratory lined with candelabra, concave lenses trapping the reflections so the flames seemed buried inside the thin glass discs like fish in ice. He loved the silence, the cold, even the stiffness of his fingers because the discomfort reminded him that he was alive and as long as he remained alive he could extend the perimeter of his knowledge a little further, could know just a little more, could see what he could see, each night something new and utterly astonishing.

He had learned the rudiments of grinding lenses from a spectacle-maker in Amsterdam. He bought his glass from alchemists and apothecaries. He made his mounts of copper and gold himself. While the people of Delft sniggered at him behind his back, he perfected his craft and after years of painstaking experiment found a method for making a magnifying lens less than an eighth of an inch across. It took him three months to grind and polish fine a single tiny lens, which he mounted with great care in a copper oblong. He was twenty-seven when he finished assembling his first microscope, yet his hands shook like an old man's. Even as he bent to look through the lens, he had a suspicion that nothing he'd seen before had prepared him for this.

"So symmetrical, so perfect, that it shows little things to me with a fantastic clear enormousness," he wrote in his diary, in Dutch. Dutch. The language of fishermen, of ditch diggers, of shopkeepers. He couldn't speak Latin, so he could not, *would not,* tell anyone about how he had invented an instrument far more powerful than Hook's microscope, an instrument that made the invisible world visible. His account would have seemed not only unbelievable but vulgar, too. Better to keep his discoveries to himself, to hoard them with a miser's devotion. He had contrived the microscope for his own use—he would relish his discoveries with a pleasure all the more intoxicating because it was secret.

Entirely on his own, for his own benefit, deriving his own conclusions, he examined shreds of cabbage, ox eyes, chicken livers, beaver hides, fingernail clippings, mustache whiskers, the sting of a flea, the legs of a louse, dry skin scraped from his arm. He took to stalking flies during the day in his dry-goods shop, climbing over counters and up shelves, trapping the insects between cupped hands and closing them in glass jars so that they died from suffocation. At first his customers stared with the scornful delight of a fool's audience, then with increasing impatience, and soon they stopped watching him at all. They left the shop without waiting for their fabric and would never have come back again if it hadn't been for Marie.

Lovely Marie, with ruddy cheeks always aglow, like her father's fine lenses. Marie coaxed the women of Delft to return to the shop, and she gave up her study of French so she could wait on the customers herself. She rescued her father's business, but not because she loved him. More than she loved her father she resented him, along with the rest of Delft believed him to be insane. But she had a strong, seventeenth-century sense of obligation. She was a daughter. Unlike her mother, who had stopped being a proper wife when her husband stopped being a husband, Marie would always be the eldest daughter of the mad lens-grinder of Delft, would cling to the identity through her father's long (sometimes she feared it would be endless) life, until he died at the ripe old age of eighty-one and she, herself an old woman of sixty by then, could close up the shop and with her small inheritance live quietly, reclusively, serving no one.

"Steady elfkin, Papa's dearest." He'd say this not to her nor to her brothers and sisters but to a dead fly as he carefully dissected its head and stuck its brain on the tip of a needle. *Papa's dearest.* What a mockery of paternal solicitude. Marie would set down his tray with his dinner and turn away in disgust, leaving her crazed father alone with his purposeless instruments.

Deliciously alone in his invisible world.

There is nothing more aesthetically satisfying than form that convinces us of its perfection, Marie's father

believed, nothing more incredible than perfection in miniature. So even if he had wanted to tell someone—and
gradually, over the years, the urge to tell began to dis-
place the urge to protect his secret—who would believe
him? He would have to tell it in Dutch. An incredible
story in Dutch! They would laugh at him, and their
laughter would seduce him like the Sirens' song until he
started laughing, too, laughing along with them, laughing
at himself.

But if he couldn't tell them, he could show them. He
had to show them before he died. Or show one of them,
one man, someone he could trust, a scientist, yes, he
knew a worthy man: Regnier de Graaf, the only man in
Delft who was a corresponding member of the Royal
Society. He was forty-one years old when he invited de
Graaf into his laboratory; he felt like a four-year-old
child, though, as de Graaf bent down to look through
his microscope at the strand of hair—Marie's hair,
which she had generously plucked for them. She
watched, too, not with her father's anxious anticipation
but with an air of disapproval, as though she were the
mother of the four-year-old boy, tapping her foot as
steadily as a clock's pendulum, waiting for de Graaf to
get on with it.

He was slow. Annoyingly slow, in Marie's opinion.
Terrifyingly slow, to her father. But when de Graaf finally
straightened his stooped back, took off his spectacles,

and wiped his rheumy eyes, he said, shaking his head, exactly what Marie's father had hoped to hear.

"Good God."

Yes, God was good. So good that after Marie's father, with de Graaf's recommendation, wrote a rambling eight-page letter to the Royal Society of London, they wrote back. The Royal Society. They had proven false many superstitions of the day, including, most famously, this: that a spider in a circle made of the powder of a unicorn's horn cannot crawl out. Indeed, it can and will crawl out, and very quickly! The Royal Society had performed the experiment themselves. Marvelous men. And these same scientists were not only interested in the lens-grinder of Delft but wanted to know more.

So he told them what he'd seen, told them almost everything. In Dutch, no less! Now when he wasn't looking through his microscope he was answering their questions, describing the "little things" in careful detail. Yet he still refused, despite the repeated requests of the Royal Society, to explain how to assemble his powerful microscope. This could wait. The eminent gentlemen far away in London hadn't earned his trust yet. He didn't trust anything or anyone he hadn't seen.

And then one night a year later, at the end of a fortnight of steady rain, he turned his instrument upon a drop of water from a cistern. Why he hadn't done this before he couldn't say—later in his life he would regret nothing as much as the fact that he'd wasted so many years examining dead and inanimate things. Because what he saw that night was more wonderful than anything else. Yes, it was the nourishment that wonder seeks: life.

He tried to restrain his passion as he wrote to the Royal Society, "I saw, with great amazement, that this material contained many tiny animals which moved about in a most amusing fashion, some spinning around like tops; others, exceedingly tiny, moved so rapidly that they looked like a confused swarm of dancing gnats or flies."

He showed no such restraint, however, when his daughter Marie entered the laboratory. He stood up from his desk with such haste that he knocked over his inkwell, and the dark liquid spread over his unfinished letter until it assumed the shape of a man's boot. Beautiful black liquid. Life in liquid. With his microscope he would examine all kinds of liquid—wine, milk, saliva, perspiration, semen, blood! He would investigate every form of liquid in the world.

He rushed at his daughter, and she managed to set down the tray with the flask of wine before he grabbed her. "Marie!" he sobbed, burying his face in her neck.

Was he weeping? Marie wondered. Had he at long last come to his senses and recognized that he'd been neglecting his family? Was this the anguish of remorse? No, he'd lost what little sense he had left, Marie realized when he lifted up his face. He was a small man and she a tall woman, so in her adult years she towered above him. She looked down on him then. He was laughing, his lips peeled back as though drawn by thread. A puppet's face made of wood and velvet, that's what she was reminded of right then, and the laughter seemed to come from a separate source across the room—from another man, a stranger, the devil hiding in the shadows, laughing for her father, through her father. And if she still fought to recognize her father in that grotesque face, she knew he was lost to her forever as soon as he spoke.

"Marie, dearest Marie. Give me a tear."

Ah, what a plaintive voice, what a pathetic man. He would always be mad—there was no chance of recovery and therefore he would never feel remorse. She despised him right then. He would never feel remorse for what he'd done to her and would never feel gratitude for all that she'd done for him. Yet she was obligated to her father, or to the demon who had taken possession of him. Without her obligation she would have been nothing. She didn't blame him for the obligation, only for his selfishness. His selfishness. Yes, for this she despised him, this mad, cloying, wooden toy of a man. She tried to push him away.

"Marie!" He held her face, brought his lips to hers, kissed her not like a father should kiss a daughter but like the devil kisses. Marie struggled to free herself. He tasted her with his thin, warm tongue and for a few horrible seconds she couldn't stop him. And then they separated with a gasp and stared at each other in amazement and mutual confusion, mirror images, father and daughter.

What had just happened?

It was Marie who understood first. She did not move, only closed her eyes so she would not have to see him. And for a moment her father understood, too. Looking at Marie, he couldn't help but understand and was ashamed. But his shame flickered and went out when he saw—*oh, gracious Marie!*—the thing he most desired: a large, milky tear that seeped from between her eyelids and slid down her cheek.

He caught the tear on the knuckle of his thumb and transferred it to a specimen slide. He set the slide on the table. While he was adjusting the glass, Marie rushed from the laboratory. He didn't try to stop her, although if he'd been her he would have wanted nothing more than to look at this aspect of himself, this expression of modesty, magnified a hundredfold. Filled with generosity, he decided that if she came back he would let her have a peek at this extraordinary image. He reached for the slide again, noticing that in the candlelight the opaque tear was the inimitable color of fire. He admired it for a moment, then positioned the slide below the metal plates, hardly able to manage even this since his hands were trembling so. Even before he had examined the tear, he started to compose in his head the letter he would write to the Royal Academy: "... an incredible number of little animals of various sorts, which move very prettily, which tumble about and sidewise, this way and that"—words of a man who had neither wealth nor fame but a success far more extraordinary, the freedom to tell the most amazing stories and to be believed. This was the lasting consequence of his invention: he had forever changed the nature of belief. Nothing visible to the naked eye could be trusted anymore, for everything had a secret microscopic life. He, the master of magnification, had made visible the unimaginable.

An incredible number of little animals of various sorts, which move very prettily. Ghosts and sylphs and demons were pale fantasies compared to these thousands of tiny worms alive in a droplet of water. Among all the minute marvels that he had discovered, this universe inside a tear would be the most marvelous of all—no more amazing sight had ever come into focus beneath the glass. To the mad lens-grinder of Delft, there was hardly a difference between discovering life and creating it.

BEES BEES BEES

Francis is fifteen years old, ill with a fever. He is asleep, dreaming, and in his dream he is crawling on hands and knees across a narrow bridge. When he reaches the middle of the bridge, he leans over the side, expecting to see his own shadow floating on the creek below. Instead he sees a man's hand and part of the arm stretching toward him——the rest of the body is a formless white mass in the murky water. As the hand glides beneath the bridge, the boy is suddenly afraid that it will rise up from the other side and snatch him from the bridge and drown him. He squeezes his eyes shut, waiting for the worst. Nothing happens. After a minute or so he blinks and peeks at the water, only to discover that he is back in his own bed, his nurse Nanette is mumbling to herself, and the sky outside the window is the flat gray of another November afternoon.

Just then, to his delight, the gray fills with snow, as though someone standing below the window had broken open seedpods and tossed up fistfuls of white puffs. It is snowing. He will not drown. It is snowing in swirls and waves. When he closes his eyes again, he sees the snow in his mind. When he opens his eyes a moment later, he sees nothing.

Bees are the souls of the dead. They are the tears of Christ. They are the offspring of the nymph Melissa, who was transformed by Zeus into a queen bee. If a bee brushes against an infant's lips, he will grow up with the gift of song. Bees are spontaneously generated in a bull-calf's crooked horn. Bees are good luck. Bees are bad luck. Bees were sent straight from Paradise by God to provide the wax for church candles. During the winter bees neither hibernate nor die—they fly to Barbary and sing the captured Moors to sleep.

Francis, where are you, Francis? Nanette is not amused. Not in the least is Nanette amused. Come out now, Nanette has something for you. Aha! There you are, you wicked boy, you thought you could hide from your nurse, such a foolish child. Leave it to Nanette to find a needle in hay. Sweet pig, here's a pinch for all the trouble you put me through, here's a pinch for mussing your clothes, and here's a good sharp pinch as a warning.

"Oh, darling pipkin, don't cry, Nanette doesn't like to see you cry. Here, Francis, here's a special treat, so wipe the tears from your face and be a soldier like your papa. My little rabbit, there's so much you don't know yet, including how ugly your Nanette is growing as she grows old, a good thing you're still too much of a baby to care. You won't despise me when you're a man, you won't ever despise me, will you, Francis? A five-year-old boy can do as he pleases but Nanette will never have a choice, no, Nanette is first and foremost your loyal servant, she's born with an instinct and will never waver, for better or worse, all her life long. Now, there's a prince, no more sobs, and Nanette will give you a reward. Close your eyes, go on, now open your mouth, open wide, and prepare to taste a miracle.

"Well? You can't tell me you've ever tasted anything so marvelous. Do you want another taste? You don't even have to say please, your smile says enough. For such a smile you will have another splendid spoonful, and another. Ah, you'd finish the whole jar if you had your way. But Nanette is in charge, she decides how much is good for you, and three spoonfuls, she declares, is quite enough.

"But you look confused. How could you know what you've tasted if you've never tasted anything like it before? You, dearest Francis, have just eaten the nectar of bees. You'll never forget the taste, will you? But I'm sorry to say this first taste will never be matched, no matter how wonderful it seems in the future. My unfortunate boy. From now on you'll want more and more, yet no matter how much you get, you'll never have enough. Like the taste of woman. Just like the taste of woman. You can blame old Nanette for the introduction!"

*F*rancis Huber was born in Switzerland in 1750. When he was fifteen years old an infection of the eye left him blind. When he was seventeen his parents moved permanently to their country estate outside Lausanne and hired a tutor to instruct him in such subjects that might be useful later in life: philosophy, theology, Latin. The tutor found the boy rather an indifferent student and soon grew bored with their daily lessons. For amusement he went fishing for trout at night.

One night Francis secretly followed the tutor. Even though he had been totally blind for two years, he had spent every summer of his life at the estate and knew the countryside intimately. He felt his way along a path about thirty yards behind the tutor, then climbed after him up the rocky slope of a hill and back down into a creek bed. He hid behind a boulder while the tutor slipped off his buckled shoes and walked straight into the icy torrent.

A few days later the tutor told him to recite in Latin. "What should I recite?" Francis asked. "Anything," the tutor said. "Make up a story." So Francis began a story about a man who went fishing at night with a lantern and club, but after a few words he slipped back into French.

The tutor didn't correct him. He described the round globe attached to a tube of metal three feet long, explained with remarkable precision how the man placed a candle inside the sealed globe and used the lantern to illuminate the river bottom. The trout, fascinated by the light, followed the globe when the man submerged it in the water and rose as he lifted the lantern. When the fish appeared at the surface, the man struck them with the club.

All the names and purposes of things Francis knew from his nurse Nanette. She was an inexhaustible source. But his tutor concluded that he was either a seventeen-year-old charlatan who had been feigning blindness, or else he was a genius. After much probing and testing, he decided that Francis was a genius and for the next few years he served as an important ally, convincing the boy's parents, despite Nanette's warnings, to indulge him in whatever he wished.

When Francis was eighteen he was given his first strawkeep of bees. By the following summer he had three separate colonies. After long years of patient study he became an expert, and with the help of a servant named Burnens he carried out a series of experiments that laid the foundations of our scientific knowledge of the life history of the honeybee.

His nurse Nanette grew senile before his reputation was widely established. He was sorry for that. She had been, however unintentionally, his inspiration through his youth. It was Nanette who had nurtured his curiosity in the world—he had her to thank for his expertise.

If a girl leads her lover past a beehive and the bees rush out to sting him, she knows that he has been unfaithful. If a man carries the bill of a woodpecker in his pocket, he will never be stung. When a swarm passes a front door, it means a stranger will arrive the next day. If a swarm lands on a house, its owner will become rich. If a swarm lands on a rotten branch, it will bring misfortune. And if a man cuts down a tree filled with bees, there will be a death in the family.

Honeybees are skilled in astronomy and long anticipated Copernicus's diagrams in the patterns of their dances. Honeybees can predict rain. Honeybees can even suck their young, completely formed, from flowers.

In general, the eighteenth century had been a dull century for science so far, in Francis Huber's opinion. In the face of the controversy over the source of life, van Leeuwenhoek's microscope was consulted with increasing determination, and now that minute structures could be observed directly, scientists set out to describe the functions of individual organs, believing that the microscope, in time, would expose the true nature of life. So science was concerned primarily with descriptive work, and the question of a special vital animating spirit was left hanging. Vitalists and mechanists alike simply kept on reading and charting the world—they'd find the answer eventually, if they were patient and persistent.

While other men made taffeta pants for toads to collect specimens of toad semen, Francis Huber was exploring the complex system inside the beehive. From the beginning of history, honeybees had been a rich source of metaphor, used by writers to reveal fundamental aspects of human nature. Francis Huber decided that if philosophers could make so many useful and expansive comparisons, he could do the same under the guise of science—eventually his research would be used to heal the human body, as truth is used to heal the soul.

He had learned from his nurse Nanette the importance of developing his five senses when he was a young boy. She had taught him how to roll a chestnut between the sole of his shoe and the ground and then to peel it with a penknife. She had fed him honey, chocolate, and milk laced with kirschwasser. She had pinched and petted and bathed him and combed his hair until it was as smooth as silk. Thanks to her, Francis was more alive— if life can be measured by awareness—than most of us, even after he'd lost his sight. Each new sensation of touch, taste, sound, and smell had its analogue in a memory that he was quick to retrieve; each new adventure evoked a vivid déjà vu, and often he felt as though he

were repeating his life. Because he seemed able to remember whatever he'd experienced, Francis convinced
those around him that he knew everything about everything. His grandeur grew as his experiences accumulated—his parents, his servant, and later his wife
considered him the genius that his tutor had announced
him to be when he was seventeen years old.

With such sensitivity to sensation, it was natural that
he cultivated the parallel faculty: imagination. With remarkable accuracy he could imagine the experiences of
others; he had watched attentively for fifteen years, and
now with a few sensory clues he could follow people in his
mind almost as though he *were* them. The cook seasoning
stew, the gardener pulling weeds, children ice-skating, his
parents sipping wine—he comprehended these in rich
particularity. Perhaps *empathy* rather than imagination
would better describe this skill. But whatever it might be
called, it was a skill that turned this ordinary man into an
extraordinary scientist. His knowledge of bees, tested
and confirmed by his servant's observations, went unsur-
passed for decades.

A genius? No, he was too steady to be a genius, too
content, too appreciative. He had no capacity for a
genius's agony. Each little discovery delighted him,
sometimes even made him laugh aloud, and opened up
possibilities of new discoveries. He spent his days imagining the life of bees and, with the help of Burnens,

comparing his imagination with the facts, facts that were like sweet tastes, like spoonfuls of honey, satisfying and enticing. Somewhere deep inside him was buried a sorrow, perhaps with a tinge of bitterness, over the great loss of his sight. But life to him was too full of pleasant surprises to dwell on what he'd lost. Life to him was sitting on Nanette's broad lap, his mouth open, his fists clenched in anticipation.

He is a handsome man now, with thick eyebrows like strips of dark, rich soil, a broad forehead and full beard. And while his build is strong, there is a lightness about him, a buoyancy, as though if he flapped his arms he would rise into the air. He seems to have no capacity for fear and so has never learned the defense of suspicion. His trust in others is complete and democratic. And even those who are conditioned to cheating won't try to cheat Francis Huber—not because they pity him but because they are afraid of his fearlessness.

A favorite pastime for the village children is to spy on him dividing a colony in two. They hide behind the hedgerow at the edge of the orchard and watch as he invites the bees to leave their hatch. Fearlessness, indeed! The blind man lets the bees crawl up his arms and burrow in his beard and hair; he chirps softly while the bees, thousands of bees, bees as thick as smoke, settle on his lips, dance across his face, wrap around his head and body as though they were trying to protect him, as though they loved him. He stands still, luxuriating in their buzzing affection, trusting them to love him, so secure in his trust that there is no danger of fear. That he might fear the bees has never even occurred to him, though it occurs to the children—they know that animals can smell fear and will strike at the first scent. This makes the spectacle of the blind beekeeper all the more exciting: if he feels even a flicker of fear while he is courting his bees, he will be a dead man.

*B*ees bees bees, that's all he could talk about, even after Nanette had taken to her bed. He was engaged to be married when Nanette became sick. She was determined to die before his wedding. She had no interest in his marriage. Nor in his study of bees. She didn't care a hoot about his reputation. What she had tried to cultivate in the boy was a sense of debt for all the years she had given to him. She wanted to be the most important person in his life and seemed to have succeeded for a short time, when he was old enough to feel adult affection but still too young to fall in love with some young tart from the village.

Both his parents had remained shadowy presences, anxious about his future but unwilling to involve themselves in his day-to-day affairs. They were scared of the boy, truth be told. Nanette knew what was what. They went out of their way to avoid him, hiring cooks and tutors and Nanette to take care of his needs and to keep him occupied. And yet despite his parents' neglect, or perhaps because of it, he had developed an air of easy confidence, as though he was sure—though not proud, Nanette would never have let him grow proud—of his importance.

Nanette knew all about importance. You can't train a cock to lay an egg and you can't expect great discoveries from a blind man. Look at all the new inventions. It was impossible even for Nanette to keep track of them: plows and threshers, steam engines, spinning jennys, barometers, lighthouses, cast-iron stoves. And this was just the beginning! There was so much Francis would never know. So why couldn't he spend his days lying by the carp pond with a sprig of grass between his teeth or clipping roses for his invalid nurse? Bees bees bees. Francis had let a gentleman's hobby grow out of proportion, and there would be no luring him away at this point. He was committed. Between his bees and his fiancée, Nanette was worth no more than fifteen minutes a day of his time.

She lived alone in a tidy cottage on the grounds of the Huber estate, and Francis would visit her with his servant Burnens at the end of each day, staying long enough to drink a glass of sherry, to inquire about her health, to ignore her complaints, and to make her laugh.

Needless to say, she didn't enjoy laughing, not one bit.

It made her bones ache and her chest sore. But he didn't bother to consider her discomfort. He made her laugh with his descriptions of the pathetic bee drones, of the fat queen with her thorax rubbed hairless by the constant licking of her attendants, of the bee workers that hover outside the entrance of the hive and fan their wings all day long to keep the interior cool. He described it in impossible visual detail, as though he were not a scientist at all, just a clever liar.

"Don't you wish you had fifty thousand devoted servants to wait on you, Nanette?" he'd tease her, and she'd say what she always said when provoked, "Nonsense," and stare sullenly at the wall. But when it came time for him to leave, she'd ask Burnens to plump her pillow, to take a blanket away or to spread another blanket over her, and Francis would have to wait. She'd think of little tasks to occupy Burnens and so delay the moment when the door would shut behind them and she would be alone again in the gray twilight, the day outside fading fast into night and every night bringing her nearer to the end.

But worse than the thought of death was the reality of the tomorrows, day after day alone with the shutters closed against the damp spring cold. She was still a tireless old woman, despite the numbness in her legs, and the energy that she couldn't expend in physical activity made her mind whirl with visions. She indulged in dreams of fifty thousand Francises taking care of her, combing her hair as she used to comb his, washing her feet, dressing her, hovering around her in case she wanted anything. Anything. Anything. He didn't need Burnens, not really. Francis was a blind man, yes, but self-sufficient, thanks to her. Dear old Nanette. Fifty thousand Francises waiting on Nanette, kneeling before her.

The only way to calm down when she'd worked herself into such a state was to repeat loudly, "Nonsense!" and make her mind blank.

*T*he egg that becomes a queen is identical to an egg of a worker. Care given to the larva alters development. An egg is laid in a special queen cup shaped like an acorn, and three days later the minute queen-larva hatches. Workers feed her lavishly with special brood food and on the ninth day the embryo queen is sealed back inside her cup, where she stretches out, spins a cocoon around herself, and turns into a pupa. During the next seven days she develops limbs, eyes, wings, antennae, and a hard shell. On the sixteenth day the young queen begins to eat away at her cell, nibbling around the top until it flaps in like a hinged lid and she can crawl out of the comb. If she is the first virgin to emerge, she tears open the other queen cups and stings the embryos to death. When she is ready to start laying, the workers will drive the old queen out of the hive. Then they will gather around their new queen and from then until her own expulsion they will groom her, feed her, carry away her waste, and defend her with their lives.

*S*he was ordinary—neither uncommonly witty nor stupid, neither plump nor thin. Like the other girls, she pinned up her braids, persistently slapped her cheeks to make them pink, longed to be noticed. But because she was the daughter of the local baker, the bread she sold was apt to take priority, even to influence perception of her, so in the eyes of her father's customers she'd been compared to a soft, round white loaf when she was just a tot and later to a firm rye, always with a streak of flour in her red hair and dried dough under her fingernails. And just as the various breads had their place on the bakery shelf, she had her place in the village. Someone would want her. One day someone would single her out, marry her, sire her children, beat her when the supper wasn't to his liking, use her and then neglect her until there was nothing left but a stale crust, food for the geese.

But she wasn't one to protest or even to contemplate a different kind of life. Along with the other girls, she was prepared to make the best of it, and since she would never have a chance to defy ordinary expectations, she set out with a fury to ingratiate the villagers with her very typicalness, to please them by blending in, by behaving as a baker's young daughter should behave, with a demureness alternately merry and dull. This pretense in itself was ordinary—all the girls were pretending, they had no choice. But they found adequate consolation in the inclusiveness of this rule. They were all pretending, they all knew it, they all delighted in their secret, a delight that was considered attractively feminine by those who didn't understand. So the girls would stand together whispering the most outrageous things to one another while the men who strolled by glanced with pleasure, charmed by their venomous laughter, which seemed as natural as sunlight. And though the older women, the mothers and grandmothers and widows, knew the truth and even felt an occasional stab of bitterness at being left out of the huddle of young girls, they didn't interfere. The harmless conspiracy would be dissolved soon enough—it was only fair that the girls should have a chance to enjoy themselves while they could.

Marie-Aimée passed her first seventeen years meeting expectations, living an ordinary life. So when blind Francis Huber entered the bakery one day, not to buy bread but to ask if she would walk with him along the river, she was dumbstruck. She had spied on him tending his bees, she had felt the same terrified fascination that the other children felt. He was a great man, and not only because he was wealthy and could do tricks with bees. He was a great man because he could not see. Among a provincial people where sameness served in place of written laws, any differences were either monstrous—

usually monstrous—or amazing. Blind Francis Huber was amazing. Pleasant to contemplate too: a grown-up cherub with the same self-absorption of a child, indifferent to his audience, carefree and careless.

With her mother's enthusiastic permission (Francis Huber was a gentleman scientist and his father was a prominent member of the coterie at Ferny), Marie-Aimée took the blind man's arm and walked out with him. He hardly needed the stick he carried. She was impressed by his sure sense of direction. And she was conscious as they crossed the village square of all the eyes on her— she anticipated the explanations she would have to give and began imagining the new title that might be hers soon: Madame Huber, good day. Madame Huber, how do you do.

But as soon as they had left the village streets behind and were following the footpath along the riverbank, she stopped thinking about what might happen and what her friends might say because she had to concentrate on discreetly serving as the blind man's guide, steering him with a gentle pressure on his arms. She hadn't noticed at what point, exactly, he'd changed his posture, tilting slightly against her, but she knew that he did so because he needed her to lead him along the uneven bank, to watch the path for obstacles, to keep him from floundering and stumbling into the river.

When they reached the base of the Jorat foothills, his

agility returned. He released her arm and clambered up a path used by shepherds and hunters. It was something to watch—a blind beekeeper climbing on his hands and knees as nimbly as a goat. And even more unbelievable was the fact that she could hoist up her skirts and follow him, unseen and unashamed. Exhilaration made her want to laugh and cry all at once. Without the familiar shame that accompanied her everywhere, that kept her humble and reserved, it was an unreal moment. She felt as though she'd been swept out of time into a fairy tale.

She never asked Francis why he had chosen her, the baker's daughter, to be his wife. At first she assumed that this extraordinary man had perceived in her some hidden distinction, but as the years passed she began to suspect that she had been chosen simply by chance, like a card drawn randomly from a deck. She was the wife of Francis Huber. A dozen girls could have taken her place.

The print of chicken feet in mud. Everywhere Nanette looked she saw the same: mud and the print of chicken feet. Thousands of tiny forked lines, though there were no chickens, nothing at all, not even a lone tree etched against the mist. She wished she were in her cottage, lying on her own bed, the fire crackling, the clock . . . but wait, she'd made a mistake! She smelled hot spiced wine, sure enough the clock was ticking, and she had a kitten on her lap. A kitten! She hated cats but was fond of kittens. This kitten could rest on her lap until it was a full-grown cat. Then she'd give it to one of the filthy village boys—he could do what he pleased with it. She stroked its head with a single finger, watched its ears flatten and its little body shudder in sleep. Maybe it was dreaming of mud, too—mud and fog and the print of chicken feet. She wondered if dreams could be passed like a communicable disease. Perhaps some dreams were more contagious than others. This dream, for example. In this terrible dream she was so weak she couldn't even squat over the chamber pot—she needed someone to slide it under her and empty her waste.

Most of the time she dreamt that she was alone—not even chickens to keep her company. Francis hardly appeared at all anymore. His wife entered the dream from time to time, though. And was here now, in fact, sitting in a chair beside Nanette's bed. Nanette was awfully fond of Francis but despised his wife and took what little pleasure she could in tormenting her. Such as: Nanette lifted the cup of hot wine to her lips, took a sip, and spit. Hah! The kitten leapt from her lap and Madame leapt from the chair where she'd been seated, cursing Nanette, using language unbecoming to a lady. A lady? Nonsense! A peasant girl, by far Nanette's inferior. She came to Nanette's cottage in place of Francis solely for his sake. But it wasn't duty that made her so obliging to her husband. Not at all. It was guilt. Nanette knew what was what, in particular that Madame had something to hide. Something to do with Burnens, eh, Madame? Something to do with midday trysts, his fingers in your hair, his tongue in your mouth. Nanette could find the secrets in a woman's face more quickly than Francis could discover the secrets inside a beehive. And Madame's face whispered that though she was married and the mother of a seven-year-old son, she'd accepted Burnens as her lover.

What Nanette knew, however, she kept to herself. Power for a poor woman depended upon a repository of knowledge. The truth about Madame would remain safe with Nanette—for the time being. Some rainy day it would come in handy, like the little bit of money she had squirreled away. It was important to put her assets to good use while she still had the strength. But she had plenty of time, more time than she'd thought she'd had back at the beginning of her illness. Too much time. Empty days. Mud and fog and chicken feet. She didn't even worry about death anymore. She'd grown bored waiting for the end, and now that Francis rarely visited, the only suspense in her life was the plot against Madame. During periods when she was sufficiently alert she would review the plot and refine it, imagining over and over the expression on Francis's face, the jealousy writ plainly on the surface, since unlike his wife, he had no ability to disguise his emotions and had never been able to hide anything from his dear old nurse.

Dear old Nanette. The contrast between her wrinkled lips and the young hand that reached out with a handkerchief to wipe away the spittle was almost too much to bear. But then she saw she was mistaken: the hand belonged not to Madame but to the young girl hired by the Hubers to take care of Nanette, to ease her passage into eternity. Wicked girl! Nanette opened her mouth and snapped, but her few teeth clacked around a bubble of air instead of around the girl's fingers. She was too quick for old Nanette. She'd better stay quick because Nanette would try again.

Where was Madame? Nanette wanted to stroke Madame's smooth cheek. Madame, the impertinent young girl announced, had gone home for the day. Nanette fell silent for a moment and then said gently, "One way to keep a girl out of trouble is to beat her black and blue." That shut her up, whoever she was. *Girl.* Nanette didn't even know her name. Come to think of it, she didn't know Madame's name either, not her maiden name. Madame Francis Huber was a stolen name. Along with the name she had stolen the reputation. But wait and see what happens to Madame's reputation when Nanette has finished with her. Wait and see.

There wasn't much more for an old nurse to do other than wait. Machines were being invented, constitutions were being drafted, experiments were being performed, and all the while Nanette sat in bed waiting for darkness and waiting for daylight. If she hadn't been Francis Huber's dear old nurse, she wouldn't have been anybody who mattered. Alone in the mud and fog. She deserved better than this. Unlike many women of her station and age, she knew how to read. And she knew the right questions to ask. On market days she had always returned with a story of some wonderful new invention. At this rate, she used to say to little Francis as she undressed him for bed, in a few years life will be effortless. But it took only a few years for her to realize the absurdity of such a notion. After all, someone must build the machines, run them, and repair them when they break down. She'd heard that in the cities the workday was sixteen hours long. Her interest in progress had waned until she scorned it altogether, and she tried her best to disillusion Francis. But it was too late. By the time he was eighteen years old, he believed that mankind had only to learn the tricks of bees in order to master the universe. As though that were the purpose: mastery. Fool's gold. Only men believed in mastery. Women believed in deceit. Ah, Nanette knew all about deceit and would turn things topsy-turvy with her knowledge. Wait and see.

When they are about three weeks old, worker bees begin foraging. They will fly up to two miles from the hive at an average speed of twelve miles per hour. Using the sun as their compass, they will visit as many as one thousand flowers, submerging themselves in the blossoms, sipping the nectar, and then brushing the pollen dust from their bodies with the stiff hair on their legs. The pollen is moistened to make a paste and then packed into pollen baskets on the hind legs. Back at the hive the workers stagger in with their load, lower their hind legs into an empty cell, push off the pollen baskets with their middle legs, deposit the nectar, and then return to work. The heat of the hive continues to condense and ripen the nectar, and when the honey reaches the proper consistency, it is capped with wax.

There was a retired jeweler, Rousseau tells us in his *Confessions,* who dug up so many fossil shells in the terraces of his garden that he came to believe that everything in the world was made of shells and the remains of shells and that the earth itself was nothing but powdered shell. He grew so impassioned about his idea that it would "finally have turned into a system in his head— that is to say, into a mania" had not a stomach tumor brought on the man's untimely death.

Francis Huber's study of bees progressed in a similar manner—albeit more slowly but in the same direction from enraptured discovery to "a system in his head." In the last years of his life his speech was disordered, his behavior impulsive and unpredictable. Before the manic stage, though, the clearest evidence of his passion was simply his tireless interest. With a wife to raise his son and elderly parents to attend to his finances, Francis Huber could spend as much time as he liked with his bees. Even when Burnens wasn't at his side observing and recording data—and Burnens, loyal as he was, couldn't be expected to share the same passion—Francis Huber continued to pursue his investigations alone. He'd sit on a bench in the orchard and listen to the industrious buzz of his bees, "white man's flies," as the Indians of America called them. He'd make mental lists of all that he wanted to know and then devise a method for his research, refine and memorize the various steps of each experiment.

He was planning an experiment to study the communication between a queen and her workers when Nanette's death throes began and Burnens summoned him to the cottage. Francis was thirty-eight years old and still relatively equilibrate in his work. So he didn't resent the interruption. But when he entered Nanette's room (he hadn't visited his poor old nurse for weeks) he was struck immediately, almost repelled, by the smell of illness, a sharp, vinegar scent that seemed to radiate not from the nursemaid's ancient body but from the porous walls.

The girl who had been caring for Nanette left her chair as Burnens guided Francis toward the bed. But Francis didn't have a chance to sit, for as soon as he was within reach, Nanette flung her arms around his neck and with astonishing strength drew him toward her so she could whisper in his ear.

The others in the room—Burnens, the girl, the doctor, Francis's wife and son—murmured among themselves, uninterested in Nanette's secrets, most likely just *nonsense*, as she herself would have said. And none of them noticed when Francis straightened and turned toward his wife, though if they had been paying attention, they would have sworn that he was actually staring at her with seeing, penetrating eyes.

A minute later Nanette began choking, and the others hurried back to her side. They stood silently around her bed, listening to her gasps as she drowned in the viscous air, all of them, even Francis, holding their breath, as though they had been submerged with her and would have to remain underwater until she died.

It didn't take long. But the sound of her final breaths—like sheets of glass being torn in two, Francis thought—was something that no one in the room would forget. Francis himself had never heard a person die before, and his new consciousness of the body's limited capacity for pain would dominate the memory of this day. Afterward, if he ever gave a second thought to the accusation Nanette had whispered in his ear, he dismissed it as a delirious product of her pain. Suffering as she was in those last minutes, how could she have known what she was saying?

*I*n the early seventeenth century, the Reverend John Thorley discovered that the king of the hive was a queen because one laid eggs as it ran across his hand. In 1637 Richard Remnant, dealer in bees and mead, discovered that the workers had female genitals. In the eighteenth century, Swammerdam was the first person to dissect bees—he made all his instruments himself, knives and scissors so delicate that they could only be sharpened under a microscope. Seigneur de Reaumur built an observation hive between two windowpanes and confirmed that the queen was the sole mother of the hive. And Francis Huber, with the help of his servant Burnens, solved problems regarding the origin and manufacture of wax, threw light on the necessity for pollen in brood-rearing, and proved that the queen mates outside of the hive.

What Francis Huber didn't realize was that twenty years before him, in Vienna, a peasant and beekeeper named Anton Janscha had already accurately described the queen's mating habits in a little book called *A Discourse on the Swarming of Bees*. But luckily for Francis Huber, Anton Janscha's work remained unknown outside of his country, while Huber's work was translated into English in 1806, catapulting him to international prominence.

*T*he years pass quietly, uneventfully, and one day he finds that he has turned into an old man. He is an old man, yes, but like a winter landscape, the surface of his body hides his mind's perpetual renewal. His ideas expand and multiply—the more he knows, the more he questions, enticed by his own confidence. Scientific inquiry is always moving forward and he moves forward with it, even while rheumatism makes his fingers ache and shingles sear his back. But there is no denying that his mind is as mortal as his body—he grows more decrepit, and the urge to find the answers to his questions grows stronger. There is so little time. His servant Burnens can't keep up with him anymore. Burnens is almost as ancient as Francis himself and much less vigorous since he lacks his master's rejuvenating curiosity. With Burnens's help Francis Huber has published two volumes of his notes and secured his place forever in the history of scientific research. Burnens isn't much use these days, though, not with his palsied hands and ears that hear only the shrillest voice. The web in Francis's mind becomes more intricate as his hypotheses remain untested.

He is an old man, with an old man's peevish whims. His parents died within six months of each other over two decades ago. He has long been estranged from his wife and son. Boredom has worked like an ulcer and finally destroyed Marie-Aimée's sympathy—she is always either irritable or indifferent. *I beg to remind you,* he wants to say, *of your origins.* They meet only at meals. If she isn't berating him for his years of neglect, she is silent and won't even partake in small talk. And his son is too absorbed in his own entomological studies these days to care about his father's research. Francis feels toward them both the same distaste that certain smells arouse. The deterioration of his love was as gradual and irresistible as the deterioration of his body. He much prefers his bees to his family. This has been true from the beginning, but now the orchard is more than his laboratory—it is his refuge.

Although he feels a moral responsibility to make his research public, he has kept one discovery to himself over the years. It is, perhaps, his most exciting discovery, so extraordinary that it would be dangerous, like Prometheus's stolen flame, if it were shared. So it remains his secret. The language of bees. Francis Huber has learned the language of bees and can communicate with them. The trick is in the pitch and variation. Bee language has its own grammar and vocabulary but is much simpler than any human language since it consists only of essentials. One must purr rather than buzz and let the epiglottis flap lightly, as though swallowing while humming.

Every afternoon in the spring and summer Francis Huber sits in his orchard conversing with his bees. The young bees come to him instinctively and settle like snow on his head. They are the daughters he never had. They are better than his own daughters, since they have not been poisoned by his wife's lies and insults.

Thirty-one years have passed since his nurse Nanette died. He's hardly thought of her since. He isn't thinking of her now, on this warm, windless June afternoon, the sky a flat white, the scene as still as a painted copy of itself. Nanette is the farthest thing from his mind. He is thinking instead about the delightful tickle as his bees crawl up his arms and around his neck. He has forty leaf-hives in all—these accordion boxes are his own design. He is hardly able to give each colony equal attention. Soon it will be time to collect the first harvest of honey. He and Burnens always do this job themselves since anyone else would be brutal with haste. Maybe Francis should let the bees keep their honey this year. No, the honey is their gift to him, they want him to have it, they've told him so. Generous creatures. White men's flies. He must keep the secret of the bee language to himself, though he is tempted to tell someone—Burnens, for instance. But it would do more harm than good. Honeybees are too selfless; other men would take advantage of them.

A slight relaxation of the larynx as air is pushed up with the diaphragm. The purr. Francis closes his eyes and thanks the bees. He can practically taste the honey and is disappointed when he swallows his own saliva. Yet despite his vivid imagination, today it is only a tease. He is so struck with desire that he stands and gropes inside a box with two fingers, rudely tears a piece of comb, and begins to slide it out.

With his hand hidden inside the accordion fold, he feels a sharp prick at the tip of his forefinger. At first he isn't sure what has happened because he can't believe it. No bee ever stung him before, not in over fifty years. This has been the main proof of his expertise. Not anymore. He understands: for the first time in his life the bees have stung their keeper. Francis Huber has been stung. He stands with his fingers inside the hive, too astonished to pull free. The bees sense his confusion and begin dancing in a panic above the hive, swirling and plunging around his head. Blind Francis Huber has been stung. It is not possible. He has been stung. As soon as the paralysis of surprise has passed, his forefinger begins to throb, and his whole body clenches in anger. He is so disoriented by this uncontrollable emotion that he believes the subsequent pricks of pain over his neck and face to be an expression of his own violent rage. He wants to kill the bees, but first he must run for his life.

*H*e was an old man, eccentric, perhaps, but famous. Although the children weren't sure what he'd discovered, they knew it had something to do with his bees. His importance was reflected in the visitors he received, wigged men who came in grand carriages from far away. It was reflected in his wife, who always wore the gently haughty smile typical of the rich. It was reflected in the manicured grounds of his estate, in the gardens, in the orchards, and, most obviously, in the swarms of bees that filled the sky over the pastures like scourges of locusts. Generations of children had watched the renowned blind beekeeper tend his bees. Spying on Francis Huber was part of the education that made a child respectful. Everyone respected Monsieur Huber. He was their local king.

So on that serene June afternoon when a group of children watched through gaps in the hedgerow as Francis Huber, barely visible inside his cloud of bees, reached with one hand into a hive, they were not only horrified when he began to scream and flail and run away. They were ashamed. For over fifty years the bees had shown their keeper pure obedience. So why did they suddenly turn against him? Because he had betrayed them—that was the only explanation possible. Because he must have broken a sacred pact. Even as they watched him run from the bees, the children blamed Francis Huber, were ashamed of him and for him, as though he were running naked through the streets while the furious people, armed with stones and clubs and pitchforks, pursued him.

NOWHERE

*I*magine a treeless landscape, marram-covered dunes and behind them flat-topped hills crusted with peat, crowberry, and heather. Down shore the seals bark, and overhead terns screech at thieving gulls. Wind hisses across the water, unfurling wisps of fog. Waves slap and rake back pebbles with a clatter. An uninhabited place, nothing man-made in sight. Nothing but the natural world, undisturbed, unmapped.

Now add a dirt lane winding down from the highlands; a copse of vestigial dwarf pine; and on a bluff beyond, a lonely stone house overlooking the sea. The cling-clang of bells tied to a skinny goat. Sheets flapping on a clothesline. A woman's angry exclamation rising above the wind: *Wicked Bill!* A man slinking off across the yard, hand cupped over his mouth to hide his wicked grin.

Clip-clop, cling-clang, whoa, halloo, halloo there! Anyone about? Halloo! A man on a sorrel mare. An ordinary man: somebody's son, somebody's brother. He is on his way to a distant port, where he will board a ship and sail to another continent and make his fortune. Respecting the conventions of his day, he has promised to send for his fiancée within five years. A young man whose mind is filled with possibilities. He looks toward the sea as he dismounts, dreaming of his adventures. Ebullient with his own promise. Not so much trusting as incautious. He aims a kick at a foraging black hen and it flies from his boot like water from a bucket. It never occurs to him that someone might be watching.

In the same grim city which the young man has left behind, a professor of anatomy sits at his desk, composing tomorrow's lecture: *You open and explore the body, you silently take in its lessons, you ponder, you see how all things are connected to one another, and with your vision cleared of disgust, you—* He stops writing, suddenly overcome by a tightness in his chest; his lungs feel as though they have balled up into fists, and for nearly a minute he cannot breathe. He drops his pen. It falls off the sloped desk onto the floor and comes to rest with its feather partially hidden by the fringe of his Turkish rug.

Forgetting in his panic that he is alone, he tries to speak, to apologize for his pain, but he has no voice; he pulls away from his desk so he may tuck his head between his knees. Old man. Sickly old man. He has devoted his life to the human body. Knows it through an intricate, associative geometry. Can follow in his mind's eye the carotid artery to the meningeal branches, the subclavian vein to the basilic vein to the venous arch in the hand. Can draw upon a board in front of two hundred students the entire circulatory system.

And now this, the body's betrayal. Deserving extreme, irreversible vengeance. He will find that hidden recess in the heart where the body lies with disease, its demon lover, he will surprise them, mockingly draw his dagger over their throats, and then plunge it up to the hilt, again, again, ripping the powerful alliance to bloody shreds, sacrificing himself to avoid the humiliation of a public collapse.

The pain fades, and the anatomist slowly regains his breath and balance. He starts to reach for his pen but is distracted by the inked lines of his lecture notes: his own didactic words, mere scratches on the soft skin of paper. Lines of black blood. *With your vision cleared of disgust . . .* This wasn't his first attack, but it might have been the worst. It means that he doesn't have much time left. Now that he can breathe freely again, the desire for revenge is replaced by the more reasonable desire to save himself, to repair his damaged heart, enabling him to devote at least another decade to charting the human body.

For his entire professional life his teaching has been restricted by priggish men who believe the dead to be as sacred as the living. Ignorance engenders ignorance, and his students have been forced back into the Dark Ages of Marinus and Galen. All they know about the human machine is what they have been able to glimpse over the shoulders of their teachers and fellows during the annual dissection. How much they could discover if the law didn't interfere. But the law will ensure that disease triumphs, the law will keep the students from great discoveries. Unless, of course, the anatomist teaches them to ignore the law.

He finds his pen on the floor, positions the nib on the paper, and continues where he left off: . . . *you will obtain a grasp of the history and cure of the disease.* He tells this to the students every year and then sends them off with their saws to carve up hogs and mongrel dogs. He resolves to change the curriculum from now on—slightly but irrevocably. The risk doesn't matter anymore. Let the law be damned!

*H*alloo there, miss. I was told I could find lodging here. Miss, wait! Miss!

She can't hear you, sir.

Oh, excuse me, I only saw the girl. . . .

She can't hear the birds. Can't hear her brother or me.
Can't hear the waves.

I'm sorry.

You're in need of a bed?

For one night. I'll be off early tomorrow. Before dawn,
if possible.

You'll not be going anywhere tomorrow, sir. There's a
storm gathering.

No matter, I don't mind a little blowing. And a clap of
thunder now and then clears my head.

Clears his head! Hah, Jenny could use a clap or two,
that's what I say. To clear her head! Can't hear the rain,
can't hear the thunder. Can't hear me and Bill doing what
we do. Pardon me, sir, but Jenny and her ears, it's a
ticklish subject. Dear little Jenny. Here's an idea: why
don't you marry her?

What?

Marry her. You'll like Jenny. I can't wait to tell Bill
I've found a fellow to take his sister off our hands. Come
on, I'm teasing. Let me show you to your room. It's a
splendid room there on the third floor. You won't complain, I wager. And later I'll send Jenny up with a pot of
tea, if you'd like. Please tell me what you'd like, sir.
Otherwise, I'll have to guess.

A young man, beard cropped close against his chin,
cheeks rising to scarlet mounds, eyes wide to take in

everything. So many novel sights. So many opportunities. It is a splendid room! The floor has been painted turquoise to match the walls. There are two paintings by the same artist, one of a wintry sea, the other of the same scene with a ship tossing about on the waves—amateurish work, yet oddly absorbing. The man ignores the view outside his window and loses himself in the painted seas, is so engrossed that he doesn't answer Jenny's knock. She enters, shuffles to the bedside table, and sets down a tray. The young man finally glances at her. Remembering the proprietress's jest, he looks her over more critically as she leaves. A diminutive thing, already slightly stooped—she'll be a hunchback before she's thirty. Poor creature, destined to spend her life in this solitary place, unable to hear and take comfort in the beat of the surf, the world's steady pulse. Such a soothing sound, yet quietly terrifying, containing in its rhythm the same fury depicted in the pair of paintings.

Outside, the sky turns a smoky blue, the sea darkens to a glossy reddish black. Inside, the young man dozes in his chair. He doesn't wake when the proprietress enters the room to take the tray away, so he misses Jenny's warning scrawled on a scrap of paper and slipped beneath his cup.

*T*o bleed a man well, hot water is essential. The anatomist watches suspiciously as his wife pours steaming water from a kettle into a bowl. He has been bled six times in the last month, for all the good it's done him, and he knows that his hand must be submerged in hot water to swell the vein. But his wife's attitude troubles him—her concern has given way to indifference, and she bustles about the room without even looking at her husband, as though she'd been hired to do the job and didn't much care about the outcome.

The anatomist's physician is more than an ordinary practitioner—he is the provost of the college where the anatomist teaches, a dapper little fellow who looks two decades younger than his seventy years. He rarely treats patients anymore but has taken on the sickly anatomist as a special project—only hastening the disease, as far as the anatomist can see. Yet he puts up with the regimen because Provost does have an extraordinary record, now more than fifteen years behind him, though during his prime he was considered the Hippocrates of the city.

Provost blames the anatomist's ill health on soups and gravy. *Soups and gravy, poisoned bait!* he says, shaking his finger, every time he visits. It's true, the anatomist likes to soak his beef in a puddle of hearty gravy, but doesn't any man? For years he has pampered his appetite in order to keep up his stamina. But he won't argue with Provost anymore; he eats only boiled apples and toast and lies passively while Provost's barber takes six good porringers of blood. This will make you young again, Provost jokes when they are through. And he orders the anatomist to stay in bed for the rest of the week. But here the anatomist refuses to concede, for he believes that work, not rest, is the surest cure. Keep a man interested in his work, and you'll keep him alive.

All the more justification to break the laws governing the disposal of the dead. Even if he doesn't find a cure, the adventure of teaching will uplift him.

*T*he young man is roused by the smell of fish cooking in the kitchen, reminding him that he hasn't eaten since noon. He sees that his tea and biscuits have been taken away. He's supposed to tell the proprietress what he would like, whenever he'd like it. Well, he wants his supper now. A more experienced hostess wouldn't wait for him to ask. But she's a peasant—they're all peasants in this part of the country, vulgar and pugnacious. Thank goodness he need only put up with them until tomorrow.

As he buttons his jacket, his eyes wander to the window. The sky has turned a sickly gray, with a strip of purple above the horizon. Whitecaps peak and froth, and off to the north a dark cloud bank presses in. A storm would suit him fine tonight. He'll stay up late reading while the flames dance in his fireplace and the rain drums against the tile roof. Maybe he'll take the time to write his fiancée a long letter describing everything—the room, the sea, the storm—so she can be here with him in her imagination.

He descends the back stairs to the kitchen but finds no one around, a pot of chowder simmering unattended over the fire. He decides to climb down to the beach and watch the storm building. Someone will surely be here when he returns.

Blow, winds, and crack your cheeks! The sea hits the shore with absolute relentlessness, like a crazed farmer beating a plow horse that has collapsed under harness. The young man doesn't feel opposed to nature—rather, the building storm draws him out of his self-interested meditations, makes him feel as though he could skip along the water's crackling surface. Spray from the waves beads on his face; his clothes and hair are pulled back by the wind, revealing his narrow, boyish frame. When he extends his arms he feels as though the wind passes through his skin and displaces the marrow in his bones.

Soon night will fall, the storm will rage. How free and impetuous, this world—and yet its dignity is never compromised. If only every man who believes himself magnificent could stand here on the beach beside him. Instead of returning to the house, he seeks shelter behind a boulder partially submerged in sea foam. He wipes his face with his sleeve. When he blinks again he finds himself staring at a smooth, oval piece of granite tucked into a crevice in the boulder.

With the guilty furtiveness of a boy stealing an egg

from a nest, the young man lifts out the rock—a wishing rock, he would have called it as a child, with a perfect ring around its center. He clutches it in his hand, watching the rain sweep across the water, wondering what he'll wish.

He remains on the beach for over an hour, believing himself responsible for witnessing the storm. He doesn't go anywhere near the barn. So he has no way of knowing what Bill does to poor Jenny, while Susan looks on.

*B*ack then: they shut patients with tuberculosis in closed rooms to ensure that they would breathe nothing but foul air. They made their stethoscopes of paper, wood, and cane. They swaddled newborns so tightly that their limbs would swell. When a man had flux, they anointed his belly with oil of quince. When a man had a stroke, they bled him and applied irritating medicines to the soles of his feet. To cure worms, they tied a piece of fresh pork to a string, inserted it into the rectum, and pulled it out, repeating with fresh pork until all the worms had been evacuated. They declared that self-pollution leaves its mark upon the face, and that women will become hysterical if their wombs are not refreshed and soothed regularly by a teaspoonful of seminal secretion. They treated scarlet fever with syrup of poppies, typhoid with antimony, and ague with Peruvian bark.

For centuries they swore by Apollo Physician that they would never, *never,* divulge their holy secrets.

If the college happens to run short of hogs and dogs, it supplies the anatomist and his students with sheep. For certain experiments, cow livers and lungs suffice. He has even made do with rats, mice, and rabbits. Once a year the body of an executed criminal is delivered to the school and is dissected in the amphitheater in front of an audience of three hundred. But his students have never worked upon a cadaver with their own hands, and the anatomist wonders, lying in bed watching the embers pulse, whether this might account for their general apathy.

Yet for the anatomist himself it was a starfish, of all things, that introduced him to the wonders of physiology and determined the direction of his life. Guided by an ancient instructor, whose hands shook so violently that he couldn't hold a magnifying glass steady, the anatomist, then just seventeen years old, had cut a live starfish into pieces, discovering for the first time the intricate system enabling nature to perform her tricks.

There are few animals as amazing as the starfish, as perfectly designed for murder. It hugs its prey—an oyster or mussel or sea urchin—and slowly forces the shell open. Then the entire stomach moves out from its body and surrounds the flesh of its victim. Digestive juices are secreted from glands in the rays, and the victim dissolves.

Children believe starfish are ornaments that have fallen from heaven. Adults, of course, know better. And will know the complexities of the human body. Starfish are starfish—the anatomist won't be satisfied with substitutes any longer. Comparative research can only tell so much. So much more still needs to be identified and diagrammed.

Margaret? he murmurs without rolling over. He cannot bear to look into her eyes, even in darkness, when he describes his plan. Are you awake? There is no answer. Margaret? He turns to face her, feeling bolder as the impulse to confess passes. Why should he make her an accessory in this crime? Yes, it is a crime, he won't deny that. It is a crime to purchase a cadaver from a grave robber and place it on the dissecting table and let his students have a go while he helps to stanch the blood with cornmeal and explains the position of organs in the abdominal cavity. It is a crime—and an act of war.

In this superstitious era the law holds testimonial medicine sacred. *Post hoc, ergo propter hoc*—After it, therefore because of it. The experimental sciences have given way to quackery, and now the majority of people are willing to believe in any foolish remedy, as long as it has a single advocate. Only a few physicians have pursued their research—the anatomist has not been among them. He has heard about an ambitious younger colleague who buys cadavers at his own expense and conducts autopsies in private. But the man has nothing to show for it, no treatise or atlas, and certainly no reputation. Through the night he works upon the nameless bodies, and by the next day he has forgotten what he has learned, too fatigued by the strain of guilt to care anymore. Or perhaps he remembers everything but is too afraid to share his information. Whatever the reason for his reticence, he has little energy left for the day's drudgeries and is widely disliked. But the anatomist expects to be spared—not by the law, he will surely be vilified and fined accordingly, but by his conscience. He will do what he has wanted to do for years, ever since he joined the faculty of the college. He will give each student invaluable experience. And maybe one or two lives will be saved because of him.

Dear Margaret. He runs two fingers over the bony clavicle ridge and beneath the lacy collar of her nightgown. He cups his hand over her right breast, still remarkably firm for her forty-seven years, since she never had a child and never gave suck. Still filled with spirit, as he is, despite his weak heart and the blood that has been taken from him. He lightly strokes the nipple, bringing it to life, realizes that his wife has been awake all along. If she were asleep, she'd be stirring by now; the pretense keeps her rigid. She's feigning sleep, squeezing her eyes shut, hoping that he'll go away even as her body concedes beneath his hand. Hers is a reluctant love, understandably, since he is a doomed man and she must prepare herself for his death. But it is love nevertheless, the anatomist tells himself as he climbs on top of her, pulling up her nightgown, thrusting into her as he holds her down by the hair, whispering—Old girl, are you awake yet?

Whispers everywhere. The blue walls whisper, the curtains whisper, the seas in the paintings whisper, no single word comprehensible, language blending into a sibilant polyphony, voices like different wind instruments playing all at once. *What are you saying? What do you want?* The strain to make sense becomes unbearable, and the young man wakes with a gasp. He knows he won't easily get back to sleep, so he wipes the stinging sweat from his eyes, lights a candle, and begins a letter to his fiancée.

I want a specimen—for research purposes. One of my colleagues notified you, I believe.

He asked us to fob a graveyard is what he asked.

Bill, the money . . .

This should be sufficient.

Aye, with that I'll buy me ten meat pies, and there won't be nothing for my wife.

Take forty, then.

What do you think, Susan?

You know the cost, Bill.

We're old hands, sir, it's a business dating back—how

long?—to the night we found those two unlucky convicts in our barn, frozen stiff.

Eight years come January, Bill.

Eight years. We've done all right, haven't we, Susan? While Jenny rides free.

Poor Jenny. Let's drink to her. Hurrah for Jenny! That's my sister, sir. An idiot. You could have her cheap.

You may have her for the asking, sir.

You know what I want.

He wants another pint is what he wants. Hey there, Sam, the gentleman has proposed another round to celebrate our transaction. We're agreed upon the price, then? Double what we've seen from you so far. And then give me your hand, sir, and we'll call the deal done. May we all prosper.

*I*t is not the middle of the night. It is the hollow in between, the dead center when time does not exist. A woman runs through the rain, her hair whipping across her face, arms flapping, mouth locked open, upper lip slightly curled as though she were crying, *caw, caw*. Her tough bare feet bounce over jagged stones. From the distance, she looks like a dollop of cream against the darkness. Flapping futilely. Oh, how she wants to rise into the air, to be sucked up into the wet night, to disappear. She runs not to escape the center but to enter it completely and forever.

What her brother doesn't realize: that she can hear everything. She hears the laughter of the water and the rocks, the chirping, playful songs of the blackbirds inside the earth's crust, the gurgle of blood spilling through a man's veins. She isn't mad. She knows too much, that's the problem. And whenever she tries to reveal what she knows, she risks her life—came close to losing it today at Bill's wicked hands, all for the sake of a cow-eyed stranger who wouldn't do the same for Jenny in a pinch, she's sure.

Wouldn't it be all right, preferable, really, to hear nothing? But already the downpour has started to ease, and Jenny can hear from the house, ever so faintly, a dead man clamoring for recompense.

*T*here are some who believe that the heart can be comprehended only by God. But with an immense effort that cost him his marriage and his career and left him an invalid, the anatomist gave five students a chance to hold a human heart in their hands. With his help, they probed its caves and tunnels, and together they made a thorough map.

It isn't until months later, alone in a seaside hotel in a foreign city, that he admits the truth: an inspection of the human body teaches nothing new. Vivisection is just as useful, perhaps more so, because the beginning of the operation can be performed upon a live animal. Every schoolboy knows the differences between the systole and the diastole, thanks to Harvey's work. By the time the anatomist had opened the chest cavity of his illegal specimen, the auricles and ventricles had hardened and a thorough dissection proved impossible—it was as though, searing hindsight tells him, he had led his students to Atlantis, only to find it demolished by centuries of war.

Remarkably, his own heart beats on, erratically at times, tormenting him with its crazy jigs but still doling out sufficient blood to keep his mind clear. His legs are so weak he can hardly walk from his bed to the terrace. But he manages this each day, and more: he has enough strength left to drink a full bottle of wine with his afternoon meal and can lose himself in the luxurious forgetfulness of siesta. His ignominy, his loneliness, his failure— all are dissolved by the fermented grape and the sun, and for a couple of hours he drowsily surveys the harbor and listens to the cling-clang of iron rings battered about by the wind.

As he moves closer to the edge of sleep, he ponders with comfortable vacuity the choices he has made: winding up here, in this Mediterranean paradise. Rather, unwinding, spinning like a top across the desolate landscape separating his home city from the advancements of civilization and finally coming to rest in the land of Dionysus, the breeze as soft as his wife's breath against his cheeks.

She deserted him not because he indulged in illegal research and subjected his name to censure, and not because he lost half a year's salary in fines. His wife left him because of his innocence. He hadn't suspected that the couple who called themselves resurrectionists were, in fact, in the business of murder, and that the body on his dissecting table belonged to a young man who surely had more of a right to the future than the anatomist did. Like a tourist in a crowded marketplace where he could speak only a few words of the language, the anatomist had had his eye on the commodity and never attempted to inquire about its origins.

So what? He's traded love and dignity and learning for the manufactured bliss of wine. What a great innovation, this refreshment, proof beyond all doubt of mankind's ingenuity. But an even greater invention, the anatomist tells himself, is the sleep that succeeds drunkenness, when the brain becomes as dense and thoughtless as a rock, and nothing matters.

*B*ill can't find his club, so he tries to stun her with the wooden handle of his pitchfork. She sees it coming and rears as he's bringing the stick down between her ears; he misses and cracks her across the nose, swipes again, and the blow caves in her right jaw. The blood doesn't pour—it drops in thick, foamy clots, and the taste makes the mare crazy. She lunges with spectacular force, ripping the iron ring attached to her lead rope right out of the beam. But her resistance makes Bill crazier—he drops the pitchfork, grabs her mane, and leaps as though to straddle her neck. The force of his weight pulls her head down, and while he struggles with all his God-given strength to keep her from bolting, Susan, who has been standing a few feet in front of them, picks up the pitchfork and plunges the tines into the mare's chest.

You'd think the horse had her first sight of hell from the way she shrieked, her huge eyes bulging, as though already the flames were flickering in the cracks between the boards, singeing her fetlocks. Moaning, legs buckling, down she goes, and Bill finishes the job with his knife. *Fare thee well, little lady.* They'll have salted meat to last them through the winter. You can measure a man's success, Bill believes, by the size of his larder. Susan feels differently. Every penny that drops from Bill's pocket she hides in an old crock, saving what she can for the day they'll suddenly have to scatter.

*I*n the beginning, she believed she owed him nothing. He hadn't even winked at her. She'd never forgotten the monk who had wandered through on his pilgrimage. He had winked at her. It was a sly, mischievous wink that said to Jenny, *Come with me.* No mistaking. That was long ago, before her brother and his wife sold themselves to the devil, and immediately after breakfast the monk had pulled his sackcloth hood over his head and continued safely on his way, unmolested, alone. Jenny had watched from her bedroom window as the last opportunity she would ever have disappeared behind the dunes.

And there was the hen to consider. Jenny's black hen flying off the toe of the stranger's boot. How she hated him right then. Cruelty marks a man more decisively than his name or heritage. And when Susan brought down the tray and Jenny saw he hadn't touched his tea, she decided that he deserved his fate.

But after the deed, when Bill and Susan had gone off to stow the body in the hay cart, Jenny was stripping the bed and found, tucked beneath a rock, a letter.

My darling Sarah, he'd begun. Nothing interesting about that, Jenny thought. But what followed was extraordinary. Another man might have written, *How my heart aches without you by my side.* Or, *Dream, my precious, of the years ahead. I will bounce our children on my knee while you read aloud, your flaxen hair glistening in the firelight.* No— for a page and a half he'd dwelled neither on himself or his journey, nor had he bored his beloved Sarah with sentimental paeans. He had written—purposelessly, as far as Jenny could tell, though with unbearable sympathy—about the inn's strange chambermaid, a pitiful girl named Jenny.

He described her as a slight, deaf and dumb creature, of pale complexion verging to bluish, who appeared and disappeared so quickly he couldn't be entirely sure she existed independently from his fancy. It was her solitude that disturbed him most. *In this bleak place she lives out her life, a poor, unwanted girl trapped within her mind. I can't imagine it, no more than I can imagine my own death.* He compared her to the mermaid from folklore who, in order to live among people, has to give up her voice. He wished he could have seen her as a little girl, half-wild, skipping and sliding down the clay bluff to the sea. *If she were a child, I would take her with me tomorrow and return to the city and put her in your care, Sarah, for she deserves to be loved. But she's clearly set in her ways and wouldn't appreciate our charity. We can do nothing for her.*

He wrote that he thought he'd seen her outside in the storm, her head of yellow hair flickering in and out of the darkness above the dunes. The apparition reminded him of one of the corpse candles that are said to appear over the River Dee the night before a person is to drown. The final line began, *I wonder what*—and had been left unfinished.

After Jenny put the room in order, she hurried downstairs and opened the guest registry and copied out the young man's address. She worked quickly, for good reason—immediately upon returning to the house, Susan ripped the page from the registry and tossed it into the fire.

Two days later, Jenny accompanies her brother and

sister-in-law the ten miles to the nearest town, a journey that they make at least four times a year. She rides in back, on top of the mountain of hay, breathing through her mouth to keep from smelling the stink that has begun to penetrate the moldering hay. They make slow progress, since their dull nag no longer heeds her master's whip and can't be urged beyond an ambling, lopsided trot. Jenny wonders whether Bill regrets butchering the sorrel mare.

When they finally reach their destination in the mid-afternoon, Bill and Susan leave Jenny to guard the cart and head off to meet their customer at a nearby pub. While they are gone, Jenny posts the letter, addressed in her own hand to the young man's home. Afterward, she climbs back up onto the hay, lies on her back, and takes the rock from her apron pocket. She holds it up against the cloudless sky to examine its silhouette and runs her fingers along its surface. It is a glossy egg-shaped stone, as perfect as though it had been carved and sanded smooth. The bar around its middle is violet, gray at the edges. She wonders what stories the rock could tell about the world under the sea, and she thinks about the stories she could tell in return.

An hour passes, and Bill and Susan still haven't returned. Jenny covers herself up to her lap with hay, hardly caring that there is still a body hidden beneath her. Eventually she falls asleep. It is the only dreamless sleep she has ever had.

As the balmy afternoon gives way to dusk and the wine wears off, he revives, and the perplexing memories once again threaten to overwhelm him: *I wonder what he whispered to his wife just before they dragged him to the gallows. I wonder whether she knew what was happening while she bucked at the end of the rope, before they put a bullet in her head to finish the job. Or does the mind empty itself of all but brutish instinct in the final moment? And the idiot-girl, I wonder whether she regretted posting that letter. Or whether she even knew, as the hangman tightened the noose around her neck, that in a few seconds she'd be dead. Or whether she cared. I don't care anymore—they should have finished me off with those scoundrels, cut out my heart and offered it to the airy nothing where superstition is born. Take it, do you hear! Take it!*

Every sunset, when the velvety band of purple constricts into a green stab of light, he expects to die. But he can't. He doesn't know how.

THE MARVELOUS
SAUCE

Cousin, she said, it was to be our last conversation, *I am going away*, her voice breaking as she took up a handful of the peas I'd shelled. She could say nothing more because right then the battle for her soul was raging, though I didn't recognize it, my poor girl's desperation, the panic in her gray eyes, and she was gone, as lifeless as our great ancestor Corneille, like him leaving behind only hollow words, *humanity, justice,* and *revenge*. If only I had understood what was happening, but no, half my attention was devoted to the sauce simmering in the pot, my marvelous onion sauce, I've never made it since, a quarter of my attention went to the peapods, so I only had a quarter left for my young cousin—Marie, as she was called by her relatives, Charlotte by everyone else.

Marie, what's wrong? I said with more than a tinge of

impatience, I confess, she'd always been one for histrionics, and imagine how I felt as I watched her squeeze her fist, destroying at least three forkfuls in one selfish spasm. And in a final act of disregard she threw the crushed peas at my feet—*Marie!*—now she had my undivided attention, *Must you behave like a child?* But the precious child, my beloved cousin, had disappeared, devoured by hatred disguised as revolutionary ardor.

There's the true assassin, if you want to rightfully condemn her—the Revolution, riding in a splendid coach accompanied by her three devoted horsemen, Robespierre, Danton, and the physician Marat, self-proclaimed Friend of the People, and my cousin is their victim, dead long before they severed her head from her body and mounted it like a pig on a pole. Did she know what she was trying to resist in my kitchen during that fleeting moment, did she have any notion of the mob's lust for cruelty as it stampedes behind the gilded coach, wild but not so willful that it isn't obedient, Revolution points with its scepter and the mob rushes in, leaving in its wake a courtyard as sloppy as a fishmonger's cart, parading along the street waving the heads of monarchs and babies?

Marie, stay where you are! I should have ordered—my bulk makes me imperious. I should have taken her by the shoulders and shaken her, I should have enclosed her in my arms, held her, crushed her, if need be, for it is much better to die from a woman's embrace than from the passion of men. See what they've done to her, incited her and then denounced her in their newspapers and pamphlets. I never even had the chance to lay her out on my marbletop like a round of dough, to sponge her pale skin and brush her hair, instead they cut off her beautiful curls and dressed her in a chemise the color of her innocent blood. I was on the terrace of the Tuilleries, I saw how willingly she walked up the stairs of the guillotine, only a poet or a saint could have remained so calm, Marie was both. Thank goodness she didn't know her favorite relative was among the multitude, for I think she would have hesitated if she'd spotted me, the matronly Coutelier de Bretteville, she would have wanted to kiss me good-bye.

I made sure that not a single person in the thousands gathered there suspected that I, the plump woman wearing black, was a cousin of the assassin and as sick with love for her as if she'd been my own daughter. I'd come all the way from Caen to see her die. She'd come all the way from Caen to stab the Friend of the People, the mighty doctor, who believed that the guillotine was the antidote of the future and set out to purge the body politic of its aristocrats and priests as he would have lopped off a leg rotting with gangrene, all for the good of the Republic. Once my fellow countrymen have tasted blood there's no stopping them—remember what they did to the Princess of Lamballe, chopped her into pieces like a fat rabbit, then washed and rouged her face and carried her head to the Queen on a platter. They were intimates, the Princess of Lamballe and the Queen, practically sisters. In less than a fortnight the decree was issued abolishing the royalty, and the King and Queen ended up on the platter, too, choucroute for the nation. There was so much blood flowing in those days that women flavored their sausages with it, but who could blame them, in times of famine those who prosper are the ones who let nothing go to waste.

I myself make a famous choucroute, unfortunately I wasn't there to collect the blood of the famous Friend of the People. Marie was there brandishing her new butcher knife—I mean *the assassin* was there disguised as my sweet cousin, wearing her favorite dishabille and a fichu trimmed with three green cords, she'd even hired a hairdresser to give her hair a dusting of powder, where she'd found the money for it all I couldn't begin to tell you—a hairdresser, the two-day journey from Caen to Paris, three nights in the Hotel de la Providence, and then the butcher knife, which must have cost at least forty sous. Why didn't she borrow one of my knives? I have a complete collection, a knife for every purpose— skinning, quartering, boning, dicing. I'm sure that among them Marie could have found one for thrusting between the first and second ribs of a man's chest, if only she had asked. But she didn't ask. She only said, *Cousin, I am going away,* crushed a handful of peas, and threw them on the floor. True to her word, she went away.

The rest of the details I know from hearsay, except the ride from the Conciergie to the guillotine along the rue Saint-Honoré, I was there to witness that, and the execution, and the burial in the cemetery of the Madeleine, where she was joined a few months later by the Queen. I wish I had been brave enough to claim her body and carry it back to Caen—on my shoulders, if need be—and bury her below the spire of Saint-Jean. From my window I can look upon the tombstones, I would have thought of her whenever the bells tolled, then and only then, in between I would have gone about my business. Instead I find myself thinking of her at any odd time: one minute I am gutting a chicken, the next minute I am standing on the terrace of the Tuilleries, both the rain and the crowd have hushed, and the blade . . .

Sometimes I stop to study my reflection in the blade, my round eyes slanted, my face stretched wide. It is the image of my opposite, who lives on the other side of the world. Everyone has an opposite, even Marie, especially Marie, we should all pray that we never meet them. Marie was introduced to the slattern Revolution over at the Hotel de l'Intendance in the rue des Carmes, where the refugee Girondins had gathered, and within a week she was possessed. Until then she'd been a good girl, a student of the nuns under Madame de Pontecoulant, who allowed her excessive liberty, in my opinion, letting her read Plutarch, Rousseau, Voltaire, and of course as much Corneille as she desired, our wicked grandfather, he put too many ideas in her head and made the sauce of knowledge so spicy and thick she choked.

Now the old manor is as quiet as a tomb, and I've developed a nervous cough simply to fill the rooms with sound. I can hardly stand it here without Marie, no one but my ancient servant Ferdinand for company. He eats just like our Chauntecleere, peck peck peck peck, pausing between bites to look suspiciously around the room and then settling on me, as though I were his property. I know for a fact that he can't taste my food—as an experiment I once stirred a spoonful of salt into his wine, of course he didn't notice. I wouldn't let him join me at the table if I didn't dread eating alone, which is why I invited Marie to come home with me in the first place; my husband had recently passed away, and the Abbaye-aux-Dames had been suppressed by revolutionary atheists, forcing Marie to return to her parents in Mesnil-Imbert. She hated the countryside, she told me so in a letter, there was nothing to do there, and, *dear Cousin,* she wrote in confidence, *Mama's cooking does not compare. How I miss your onion sauce!*

That touched me, I admit. For her first dinner I prepared chestnut soup, squabs stuffed with veal and roasted in a salt crust, potato cakes, and of course my onion sauce. The next day she painted me a little picture of two Cupids surrounded by garlands of roses, signed Corday. I often thought about how on the day of my funeral she would drift sadly through the house, and she'd come across this picture and remember our dinner. It was a comforting thought, imagining my little cousin savoring a memory of me.

Instead she threw the peas on the floor and kissed me and left—to visit her family, I assumed, when really she had engaged a place in the diligence for Paris, intending, God forgive her, to slaughter the Friend of the People. If only he had stuck to his optical investigations, this never would have happened, I would have kept my Marie and he would have kept his life and France would have kept her wits. Now I have to light candles in Saint-Jean for all three, penitence is my obligation, since I am guilty, too, guilty of selfishness. The world was changing and I was too much of the gourmand to notice, I just kept shelling my peas while Marie rushed from the kitchen and into the courtyard, where she almost fell over tiny Louis, the carpenter's boy, who was playing with his new puppy. According to him she bent down, kissed him on the forehead, gave him her sketch pad and pens, then disappeared before he could thank her.

That was the morning of the ninth. On the fifteenth Ferdinand read to me the first report in the newspapers of the assassination. The trial was set for the morning of the seventeenth. No matter how hard the driver whipped his horses, he couldn't get me there in time, the members of the Tribunal in their black cloaks and black hats decorated with tricolor plumes had already condemned my little cousin and sent her back to her cell to await death. For all I know they dined magnificently afterward, quail eggs and chateaubriand was probably the fare, though the rest of the city was starving. Take it from me, the highest priority for a Revolution deputy was his appetite, and by the time he'd sung the Marseillaise six or seven times, he was crazy with thirst.

Meanwhile, my fearless little cousin, a touch vain to the end, spent her last three hours sitting for her portrait, she wouldn't even eat her final meal, so I'm glad I didn't risk my life to bring her the mulberry comfit I had hastily prepared before I left Caen. I never had the chance to speak with her again, for when I reached the door of the Conciergie and saw those guards standing with their gleaming swords unsheathed, courage failed me, I feared that if I identified myself they would have accused me of being a collaborator and taken me into custody, I wouldn't have seen the light of day again, much less my kitchen, they would have left me to rot in some dungeon like a potato.

So I turned my back on the prison and my cousin and set out to gather all the information I could. The details were as various as flavors at a feast——I sampled a different version at every street corner. All of Paris had been listening for days, now they wanted to tell what they knew, so for the afternoon I was the most desirable of guests—I had traveled hundreds of miles, I told them, to be present at the great event, the execution of Charlotte Corday. They invited me into their shops, they offered me a chair, they poured me a glass of wine and brought their faces so close to mine that I could see my own face in the pools of their eyes.

Madame, they began with great solemnity, *across the river in the Faubourg Saint-Germain, on the rue des Cordeliers, lives the Friend of the People.*

Lived! a voice would interrupt. *He lives no more!*

What they told me was already everyone's business, I could have spared myself their paltry hospitality and read the official account in the newspapers: the sabot-shaped bath, Marat with a vinegar-soaked handkerchief around his head, a map of France on the wall, two pistols above the map, a plaque above the map with the words *La Mort.*

La Mort. People never failed to remark upon the coincidence with a shudder, Marat's fate spelled out in six letters above his head, as for the hundredth time they told what happened, how on that fateful morning at nine o'clock a pretty dark-haired girl managed to creep past the concierge and tug the iron bell pull. Or she didn't manage this at all, some insisted, in fact the concierge blocked my cousin's way, told her that Monsieur was not receiving visitors, ordered her to leave at once. So Marie retreated and came back a second time a few hours later, slipped past the concierge, rang the bell, and informed the doctor's mistress, who opened the door, that she had an urgent message to deliver. Or the maid answered, according to others, and Simonne, the mistress, appeared after she heard a strange woman's voice, and she told my cousin that it would be useless to return.

But what does the order matter? The end is always the same, though there is still speculation about whether or not my little cousin acted alone. Certainly she had no one with her when she returned a third and last time at seven-thirty and pushed her way into the antechamber and was invited into the salle de bains by Monsieur Marat himself, who believed what Marie had told him in a note, that she had information about the plotting Girondins in Caen. Who would have thought my little cousin capable of such a shrewd maneuver? Probably she was as surprised as anyone when she found herself face to face with the famous man, who lounged stark naked before her, as oblivious as a side of beef to a woman's modesty, the skin on his chest patched and peeling, his indifferent sex hidden only by the writing table strapped across the bath. You have to admire Marie's calm as she bided time with lies about the supposed rebellion, waiting for Simonne to leave, which the mistress finally did after giving her master his carafe of water with almond paste and clay mixed in, taking with her the plate of sweetbreads and brains.

Isn't it strange that a man with Marat's influence would prefer clay to the delicate organs of a calf? Which only proves that he was the coarsest of heroes, even when he had a choice he swallowed spoonfuls of dirt, certainly there was plenty to go around with all the graves they were digging in those days. But to his great surprise he was compelled to sample another concoction that day, a dish called Peace prepared by my own cousin. She had brought with her nothing but a sharp knife and a measure of foresight, and look at her achievement! Marie may have followed directions to Marat's door, but the rest she made up all by herself, a technique she learned from me.

Her mistake, though—and I would have told her this if she had asked, of course she never asked—was to serve the meal without sending invitations first. There were no sympathizers in attendance, no one to appreciate her courage. All by herself she plunged the knife into the right ventricle of Monsieur's heart and then turned and ran into the bedroom, where she was felled with a chair thrown by one of the servants.

I don't like to think of my cousin as she was led down to the street and through the jeering crowd. She believed she'd rescued the nation, they called it murder and murdered her. Even her own parents issued a statement three days later declaring that Marie-Charlotte deserved her punishment. I will say one thing to recommend the guillo-tine: it is efficient. And now we may all breathe more easily because, thanks to a whim of justice, the despots Danton and Robespierre followed close on my cousin's heels and were executed within fourteen months. With-out loving friends to care for it, the neglected blade has begun to rust, like any knife it needs to be cleaned and sharpened regularly, soon it won't be able to split an apple in half.

I wonder what became of the butcher's knife my cousin used to kill the doctor. I couldn't very well have marched right up to Fouquier-Tinville, the Public Prosecutor, and declared that I had first rights to the knife, though I would have liked to add it to my collection. I would have saved it for only the most formidable jobs, dismembering a goat, say, I prefer to do this hard work myself since the butcher always manages to mangle the delicate flesh around the joints. I don't even have the final portrait of Marie in my possession. I returned to Caen hungry and empty-handed but with a head full of the horrors that I'd witnessed, and in an attempt to forget them I've kept myself occupied cooking elaborate meals for myself and my ungrateful servant Ferdinand, soups and roasts and pastries. As I've said, I haven't made my onion sauce since I prepared it for Marie. I'm certain the taste would remind me of her, though so many years have passed I can't recall exactly what she looked like.

It's amazing I've grown so rotund and still keep growing—I am wider than three Maries. Even so, I manage to travel by myself to Paris every summer, I wander the streets and visit the Tuilleries on the anniversary of my cousin's death. And each time I understand afresh that I've come all the way for nothing. So at the end of the day I sit on a bench beneath a peeling hickory tree in the cemetery of the Madeleine and weep soundlessly. Usually no one bothers me, and when I am through I dry my eyes and go back to my hotel.

There was a difference on this last visit, though—an unanticipated interruption. I didn't even notice the peacock until he sauntered across the path and spread his brilliant fan for me, and then as I wiped my eyes he tilted back his head and shrieked.

Have you ever heard a peacock shriek? I used to think it the strangest sound in the world. But there is one sound stranger, it came unexpectedly from within my own throat on the day my cousin was executed. I wasn't aware I could make such a sound—a bird, yes, but a woman! Believe me, I would have kept quiet, I have had a great deal of practice being stoical through my life and I was ready for the scene, I'd gone through it in my mind at least a dozen times while I waited for the end, the blade falling, the head dropping forward and the body slumping back, all the blood. But I was not ready for what happened next.

I've always known that people can be hateful, how

hateful, though, I didn't comprehend until I watched along with five thousand other loyal citizens as a man leaped onto the platform and fished my cousin's head from the basket and held it up by the hair and slapped her face. That's when I made the sound stranger than a peacock's shriek. Fortunately none but my closest neighbors heard me above the murmuring crowd, which was all the slap provoked from the rest of my fellow countrymen, I'm ashamed to say, a civilized murmur, a blush of sound. I stole off before someone could put a hand on my shoulder and demand an explanation for my outburst.

To tell the truth, as often as I've come back to that final moment when nothing moved but the blade—and in my mind even the falling blade is suspended interminably—I hadn't thought of that slap with any clarity for years and years. But the peacock in the cemetery of the Madeleine reminded me. Still, the worst was over in a matter of seconds, I stopped trembling and stared that impertinent bird right in the eye and pictured him roasted and stuffed, fragrant juices running clear as Ferdinand carves the first slice, my own mouth watering. I've never tasted peacock, but I hope I have the opportunity before I die. Imagine: tender white peacock meat cooked to perfection, brilliant peacock feathers in my hair. It will be my finest creation. For such a meal I will even make my marvelous sauce, the aroma will fill the old manor and lure a flock of angels down from heaven, perhaps Marie-Charlotte will be among them wearing diaphanous white, her nostrils puckering. I know it isn't likely, but just in case I shall leave a window open and put another setting on the table. It will be the final measure of my expertise.

CHLOROFORM JAGS

In the mid-nineteenth century, in the little town of Tucksville—a town hardly changed even today, where you'll still find the same frothy cupolas crowning the same houses, the same three-story inn baking popovers from the same secret recipe, the same family names painted on mailboxes—women were begetting at a furious pace. Children swarmed lawlessly through the streets, tumbling over one another and ignoring all warnings and prohibitions. In summer they took turns diving from the ledge of a thirty-foot-high rock into Dill Creek, in winter they skated on the thin ice of Lake Keetlecoe, sacrificing one or two of their companions every year to the perils of play. Which only encouraged their mothers to conceive again because life was so dangerous and the survival of the young so uncertain. The population multiplied as fast as the local millinery spit out hats, and sometimes the poor midwife didn't have a day of rest for weeks at a time.

What Miss Agnes, the midwife, did with all the money she must have accumulated was a constant source of wonder. Some said that she'd buried her savings in a sack in her yard and then forgotten where she'd hidden it. Others claimed she'd dumped her money into the lake in a fit of private rage—a rage that all spinsters suffered, according to the wisdom of the day. But unless Miss Agnes was attending a birth or working in her garden, no one knew how she spent her time or what she'd done with her fortune. And though later they'd regret their cowardice, no one dared to ask.

She lived most of her life in a small clapboard cabin on the south shore of the lake. Her mother had died when she was three days old of puerperal fever; her father, a blacksmith, ran off with the wife of an itinerant preacher when Miss Agnes was twelve, leaving her to fend for herself. Although the town was willing, she refused any permanent help. She let it be known that she would not be taken in or kept or reared or raised. But she did accept frequent handouts, arriving unannounced at dinnertime at any random home or sitting in front of the apothecary's with a cup for pennies at her feet. And three or four days out of the month she would appear at the local school, so the teacher always kept a desk free for her. The town grew accustomed to her gypsy ways and even came to consider her something of a local treasure to be coveted and protected, like a martyr's reliquary or an ancient, jeweled crown.

Then she disappeared. One afternoon in March Father Cecil noticed the door to her cabin swing open in the wind, and when he shouted for her there was no answer. She was eighteen years old when she left Tucksville, gaunt and ugly, with black slivers for eyes, a harsh jutting jaw, and such a small head on her elongated neck that you couldn't help but think of a chicken when you looked at her. Yet no one had ever taunted her with nicknames. She'd been called Miss Agnes from the day her father had taken flight and would always be called Miss Agnes, even in her absence.

It was an absence that caught everyone by surprise: she probably hadn't meant to, but by slipping off without a word, Miss Agnes left the town as confused about itself as if it had misplaced the official registry of births and deaths.

The purpose of chloroform is not to escape time but to dissolve time, to exist in an infinite present, cheeks burning, eyelids as slippery as buttered wax beans, the mind disconnected from the setting, the body no more a part of you than the red velvet wingback chair in which you sit, your chin tipped against your chest, your feet propped on the ottoman in front of the hearth. A chloroform jag is not sleep—a sleeper has some consciousness of the hours slipping by. It is much closer to death: a dream of death. Whoever invented the notion of hell did not understand pain. Pain depends upon time passing—there can be no such thing as eternal pain because the body will become indifferent to anything permanent. Pain cannot be constant, even in the afterlife.

There is no afterlife, Agnes has discovered. There is only death and the dream of death. She is dreaming now, in the infinite present. When she wakes her eyes will seek the clock, focus on the face, study it until she can remember what it means.

She has made pain her life's study, freedom from pain her ultimate goal. She used to experiment with the drug upon rabbits and cats. Now, because her research has progressed so far, she experiments upon herself. She's convinced that she has nothing to fear, for if she makes a mistake she'll never know it.

At first the town thought Miss Agnes had drowned—footsteps in the wet snow led from her yard onto the ice of the lake, ice that sagged and cracked beneath the weight of the sheriff when he walked out tentatively a few yards. So nobody attempted to follow her trail. They could only wait for the ice to melt and for poor Miss Agnes's body to wash up onshore.

But spring arrived without Miss Agnes. Nor did she or

her remains appear that summer or fall. Her lovely garden went to seed, and young boys took turns throwing stones through the windows of her cabin. Not until the following March, exactly one year to the day after she had disappeared, did Miss Agnes return—in the dickey of the mail coach this time, sitting as straight as a newly elected politician, a raven feather in her hat and a tight-lipped smile on her face. She moved right back into her cabin as though she had only been gone for a week, and she spent the rest of the afternoon tending to her home and the evening posting broadsides on trees and lamp-posts.

Children walking to school the next day were the first to read Miss Agnes's proclamation; they ran home and dragged their parents out to read it for themselves. By noon the town of Tucksville had concluded that if Miss Agnes wanted to set a new ordinance, there would be no stopping her.

Printed on the broadside and signed by Miss Agnes was this: "It is ordained that no woman within this corporation shall exercise the employment of midwifery until she has taken oath before the mayor, recorder, or an alderman, to the following effect: that she will be diligent and ready to help any woman in labor whether poor or rich; that in time of necessity she will not forsake the poor woman and go to the rich; that she will not cause or suffer any woman to name or put any father to the child, but only him which is the true father thereof, according to the utmost of her powers; that she will not suffer any woman to pretend to be delivered of a child who is not indeed, neither to claim any woman's child for her own; that she will not suffer any woman's child to be murdered or hurt; that she will not administer any medicine to produce miscarriage; that she will not conceal the birth of bastards."

The following Sunday Miss Agnes, in front of the mayor and most of the town, was sworn in as Tucksville's first professional midwife, a role filled previously by sisters and mothers who had done what they could to ease the laboring woman's pain until things got out of hand, and then they'd call the doctor. But nineteenth-century American husbands were still uncomfortable with the idea of another man peering between their wives' legs, and they were the first to welcome Miss Agnes as a preferable alternative: a female with a physician's skill. If from time to time Tucksvillians remembered the ragamuffin she used to be, they treated the memory like obsolete currency—her past had no meaning now that Miss Agnes was a professional, with a certificate to prove it.

Perhaps it was the convenience of having a full-time midwife in town, perhaps it was merely a coincidence, but right about the time Miss Agnes returned from the city, the trend of childbearing accelerated. Women who were grandmothers suddenly conceived again, girls who hadn't yet learned to sew grew as round as their mothers. One woman gave birth to seventeen children in as many years. The urge to reproduce was as insistent and mysterious as the urge to fight a war—once it had started there was no stopping the momentum.

So time passed, the town filled with children, and Miss Agnes grew rich. Except for her garden of extravagant hybrids—roses far more fragrant than ordinary roses, lilies and irises much larger and more brilliant than others of their kind—she continued to live simply and penuriously. But the town believed a rich woman obligated either to share her wealth or to flaunt it; no bad character was held in more contempt than a miser. Tucksvillians began to wonder whether she was a miser, and if there hadn't been a dramatic change in Miss Agnes's life, sentiment might have turned against her. But as it happened, one day Miss Agnes was seen walking along Main Street carrying a baby girl in a picnic basket. She told the people who clustered around her that she had gone to the woods in search of early fiddleheads and had found the infant swaddled in a tattered green cloth lying in a patch of snow. She had carried the baby in the hammock of her apron back to her cabin and had set her to thaw beside the fire. While she spoke, she let the child suck on the knuckle of her forefinger, and she was so jubilant that no one cared to remark upon the strange coincidence. Coincidence, indeed! What Miss Agnes really had found was a young woman in trouble. It was such an obvious story that people didn't mind the midwife's lie.

She named her Myrtle after the hardy plant that pokes through the snow all winter long. Despite the law, which in the absence of relatives normally appointed the state as guardian of an abandoned child, Miss Agnes raised Myrtle as her own.

*H*er own heart pumping beneath her skin, red coals pulsating behind smoke. Far away the King of Spain sits down to a meal of roast suckling pig. In the mansion at the top of the slope, the industrialist Quinby, owner of the millinery, mounts his wife. Somewhere in the forest an opossum hangs by its tail from a branch, its copper eyes shining in the darkness. And in Agnes's cabin, a girl stands outside a bedroom door, her face pressed against the keyhole.

Chloroform has removed Agnes so far from the constraints of the body that she sees what she cannot see: from Spain to the other side of her bedroom door, where a girl is spying on her through the keyhole. A girl and a keyhole. How much does she know already? How much, Agnes wonders, does she want to know?

Agnes is not supposed to care about anything during this dream of painlessness. But she cares that the girl is watching her, staring her back into time. *What are you doing in there, Miss Agnes?* She is doing nothing. She is nowhere doing nothing, unable to move or speak. The girl is watching her. If she could, Agnes would call out and tell the girl to go away. But she is helpless.

*M*yrtle entered the life of the town from the outside— no one entirely forgot that she was a stranger. Yet time dulls apprehension, and Tucksvillians grew used to her, children treated her like a favorite pet, adults pinched her cheeks and kissed her. She accompanied Miss Agnes to every lying-in, and by the age of ten, she knew the stages of labor as educated girls her age knew the multiplication tables.

If asked about herself, she would insist that she was different in just one way: most children came into the world in a bloody mess, but Myrtle believed that she had been sown by her natural mother in the forest when she was a tiny seed. She must have shrieked when Miss Agnes plucked her, just like the flowers shrieked when they were cut. True, Myrtle had never heard the flowers, but that was because she sang loudly whenever she snipped a blossom, as Miss Agnes told her to do.

Women in labor shrieked and moaned for God, which was why Father Cecil and other clergymen feared that relief in any form would rob childbirth of its dignity and God of those deep, earnest cries for help. So Miss Agnes kept her supply of chloroform a secret. The sole comfort she ever dared to offer was the conventional bottle of whiskey, which she hid in her apron, where she had once carried Myrtle. She presented the bottle to the mother-to-be only if there was no physician present, or, in extreme cases, when his back was turned. Miss Agnes's whiskey didn't do much good, though. Women usually preferred pain to eternal damnation, crying out for mercy instead of relief.

To those who had never been witnesses, birth was an awful and wonderful mystery. Young children would gather around Myrtle after a baby had been born to hear an account, though they knew that no matter how eagerly they pressed, Myrtle would continue to guard her knowledge with a sense of responsibility far beyond her years. She had spent her childhood at the midwife's side; she emerged from every lying-in veiled by the same wise and secretive expression.

Miss Agnes brought Myrtle with her because the sight of the young girl reassured the mothers and also because Myrtle was supposed to learn the trade. If the baby was slow in coming, Miss Agnes sent for the doctor, despite the husband's modesty. Sometimes the baby never came, and the exhausted woman would fall into a sleep so deep that nothing could wake her, not a bell, not a prince's kiss, not even Dr. Stanforth, who always knocked his forceps against his medicine chest three times for good luck before inserting them into his patient. It was only then that Miss Agnes would take Myrtle's hand and lead her from the room.

*S*he is staring at the clock. What went wrong? She can't remember. She has not regained consciousness—she has lost senselessness and now is back where she started, in the red velvet wingback chair with her feet still propped on the ottoman, the soles of her shoes hot from the coals. What can't she remember? She's left with a vague, troubled feeling, no images from the lost infinity. Her anxiety is like a bird trapped in a lightless room, its wings thrumming against the walls. She will have to return to nowhere again in order to free the bird.

She reaches for the tumbler of chloroform on the table beside her and sniffs the invisible vapors rising from the liquid, then douses a handkerchief and holds it beneath her nose. Before senselessness there is a wave of exhilaration, all the more pleasurable because it is the assurance that painlessness will follow. As the wave recedes, she folds her arms and cries, "I'm an angel! Oh, I'm an angel!" Then she feels nothing.

*M*yrtle wore her hair—brown, with a tinny, almost bluish shine to it—straight to the middle of her back. Her round black eyes gave her a look of somber innocence. Her cheeks were as velvety as the petals of a tulip.

The girl thrived upon Miss Agnes's diet of boiled goat's milk, gruel, peas, lettuce, almonds, and white bread, and the more lovely she grew, the more credit Miss Agnes took, and received, for her adopted child.

And Myrtle returned Miss Agnes's doting pride with devotion, even worship. When they were attending a lying-in, Miss Agnes had only to glance at Myrtle and the girl would know immediately what was needed: hot water, a clean towel, scissors. People would have forgotten that these two were not related by blood if Miss Agnes hadn't been so ugly and Myrtle so beautiful. But because of the contrast, everyone remembered all too well that image of Miss Agnes carrying the basket with a baby nestled inside, a baby no bigger than a corncob, and every mother in Tucksville was privately envious, wishing that she'd been the lucky one to have received the child as payment for services rendered. How easy it had been for Miss Agnes, compared to other women; how wonderfully simple, her blessed surprise; how effortlessly the child had been acquired.

When they were alone together Miss Agnes would tell Myrtle about such fantastic things as singing heads floating in a well or the little people who rode down from the sky on the backs of snowflakes. But Myrtle's favorite story was her own: the story of a girl rooted to the forest floor, sprouting up through the snow. Tucksvillians may have thought Miss Agnes lucky to have discovered Myr-

tle, but Myrtle insisted that she was the fortunate one to
have been found by Miss Agnes, who hadn't stuck her in
a vase to let her wither and die as another woman would
have done but fed her, educated her, told her stories, gave
her her own pretty gingham apron. Yes, Myrtle was
grateful to Miss Agnes and for twelve long years remained devoted.

Sliding. She wants to reach out and clutch something
fixed, but her arms are too heavy to lift. So she continues to slide across the open space of her room from
the red velvet wingback chair toward the door. She is
moving so slowly and so rapidly at the same time, as
slowly as the sound of her breathing, as rapidly as light.
Sliding. Only when she is a finger's length away from
the door does she notice the knob, its slanted glass
planes reflecting the flame of the oil lamp. Sliding. The
flame is wriggling, dancing, and the doorknob is rattling.
Wait: the flame is burning straight and the doorknob is
still. Now the flame and the doorknob are dancing again
and Agnes is sliding from her chloroform jag back into
time. Across the room the flame in the lamp is burning
straight, but here, a finger's length away, the glass
doorknob is shaking. The whole door is rattling.
Agnes's eye is reflected twenty-seven times in the doorknob. Count them: twenty-seven eyes. Sliding. She is
sitting in her wingback chair and the doorknob is shak-

ing. Does someone want to come in? Come in, then, come in. Agnes has nothing to hide.

*O*nce a year, ever since she'd adopted Myrtle, Miss Agnes would leave her goddaughter and travel eighty miles to the biggest city in the state. She would return a fortnight later with a large wooden box balanced on her lap. Tucksvillians believed the box contained pips and bulbs of the rare hybrids that filled her garden. Only much later did they learn the truth: that Miss Agnes went to the city to purchase chloroform, that chemical considered by local authorities not only morally pernicious but deadly as well, despite Queen Victoria's personal endorsement. More than one woman had never woken up from her chloroform sleep. So even if she had tried to tempt the mothers of Tucksville—and by all accounts she never had—they would have scorned the drug. *In sorrow thou shalt bring forth children* was still the order of the day.

It was Miss Agnes's own devoted Myrtle who revealed the midwife's secret to the town. The green shoots of daffodils were still slick with dew on the spring morning when Myrtle saw Miss Agnes off on her annual trip to the city. In past years the girl had returned alone to the cabin and remained there for the entire two weeks that Miss Agnes was away. But this year Myrtle had other plans. And though Miss Agnes seemed distracted by the impending journey, surely the odd expression on Myrtle's face didn't escape her. The girl's delicate features were pinched; her eyes were puffed from too little sleep. The trouble had arisen the night before, during an intimate conversation between the midwife and the girl. Miss Agnes had let the truth about her birth slip out, and now her goddaughter would never forgive her. When she kissed Myrtle softly on the lips, she knew it was for the last time.

Myrtle waited until her godmother was out of sight, then she gathered the folds of her hood under her chin and hurried to the nearest house. From the front yard she called the names of the two children living within, inviting them to come out to play. She did the same next door and on down the street until she'd assembled a troop of children. Then she led them to Miss Agnes's home, singing patriotic songs and clapping the entire way.

But though they willingly paraded after her through town, her young crusaders faltered outside the door of the cabin—no one other than Miss Agnes and Myrtle had ever been inside, and the children were afraid of what they'd find.

They'd find chocolate dollars and licorice, Myrtle promised them. They'd find porcelain beads and marbles and oyster shells. The lucky one would find a jar full of pennies. It was a treasure hunt with prizes for everyone; she convinced them that there was no reason to be frightened.

Tentatively they entered, but within minutes they were stomping and whooping through the cabin, in a frenzy they smashed teacups, overturned mattresses and tables in their greedy search for the promised treasures. And treasures weren't their only goal—Miss Agnes, the midwife of Tucksville, had been a kind of divine handler in charge of the mystery of birth, and by making the cabin their own, ravaging it, disassembling it piece by piece, the children could explore the mystery. There was no one to scold them for their childish wonder. Before they were finished, they would know everything.

A few hours before the break of dawn, Agnes sits across from her goddaughter and admires the child's creamy, heart-shaped face. The difference between them is as vast as the difference between the two states of consciousness. Miss Agnes is in a very strange mood tonight—the girl says as much, and Agnes bursts into laughter. Innocence has never seemed so hilarious, or, with her next breath, so pitiful. Agnes stops laughing. *The journey from the known to the unknown demands complete resignation,* she explains. Agnes understands all too well the extent of the commitment entailed. You must give up the familiar. You must be prepared to give it up forever. Which is not to say you won't return—only that the risk is great.

So does Myrtle want to try? Is she prepared?

*T*he solution to the mystery was really very simple, the children learned. After half an hour a group decided that there was nothing valuable to be discovered in Miss Agnes's closets and cupboards, so they went to see what lay below. They broke through the lattice beneath the front steps and crawled under the porch, where they found what they might have expected: spiders and grubs, an old wooden bread box, a vinegar bottle, a rusty spade. One little girl grew bored, took up the spade and began idly scratching in the dirt. She wrote her name, digging deeper ruts to mark the first letter, a capital *A* for Anna. In the bar of the *A* the spade clinked against what she thought at first was the jar of pennies but turned out to be a bone. Not just any old bone. It was a human bone still animated by a spirit— once she'd scraped the dirt away, it bent forward and beckoned her to come closer.

A simple solution. So simple that poor little Anna began to howl, which scared the other children beneath the porch. A boy tried to leap up, knocked his head against a beam, and burst into tears. The panic spread to those inside the cabin. They screamed for help, all of them certain that something horrible had happened and that they wouldn't live to tell about it.

The sound of their hysteria traveled along the shore to town. Adults looked up from whatever they were doing, cocked their heads, recognized the voices, and began running in the direction of the screams. This wasn't the sound of one or two little souls flying up to heaven—this was an entire generation.

As the parents arrived at the cabin, children rushed into their arms. No matter that a mother wasn't matched with her son or daughter—to clutch any child securely was enough. Finally the sheriff appeared and somehow managed to locate in the mayhem the little girl who had started it all. And when he himself had crawled beneath the porch and identified the source of the panic— "Nothing but a knucklebone," he announced—the parents were so relieved that they cheered the sheriff for his good work.

He was wrong, however, about the "nothing but." The knucklebone was attached to a hand, the hand to a wrist. As the clamor faded, the deputy and sheriff unearthed the remains of a human being and dragged it from the crawl space into the sunlight. The people gasped, drawing into their lungs the mild spring breeze hissing through the trees.

So this was how the town discovered that the midwife of Tucksville was a thief, that twelve years earlier she had stolen a child from the waiting hands of God. Some people whispered even as the remains were dragged into the open that Miss Agnes had murdered the woman and boiled and eaten her before burying the bones beneath the porch. But Myrtle, looking almost pleased with herself, said that wasn't true at all. She assured the people that her mother had died of natural causes, and that Miss Agnes had split her open only after she was dead. Her godmother had confessed the whole story to her the night before she'd left for the city. And if anyone cared to know why Miss Agnes really went to the city every year, they had only to follow Myrtle to the garden shed, where three full vials of a clear liquid, Miss Agnes's magic potion, were discovered, along with dozens of empty vials in a bushel basket.

According to Myrtle, the young woman had come to Tucksville from a distant town. One bitter March night she'd appeared on Miss Agnes's doorstep, panting and groaning in the final stage of labor. But complications had arisen, and before Agnes could run for the doctor, the woman's weakened heart had given out. Within seconds, Miss Agnes had performed the brutal operation. She'd used a kitchen knife, Myrtle told the sheriff. She'd cut open the swollen belly and plucked out the baby. And then, ignoring her own edict, she had claimed the child as her own.

The experience might have driven Miss Agnes insane; instead it drove her to chloroform. She had vowed to herself that she would find an antidote for pain. Through her chloroform haze she'd told Myrtle, *Soon women will no longer suffer like your poor mother suffered.* After extensive research, she was ready for the day when Father Cecil and Dr. Stanforth changed their minds about chloroform. They would come around, she was sure of it. The whole world was coming around, and Tucksville would have to follow.

*I*t is a supreme union, this shared chloroform dream, far more magical than the act of love between a man and woman, approaching, perhaps, the union between a mother and her unborn child. But it isn't blood they share; it is the state of senselessness—the two minds wandering through red, liquid light, compressed into one, inextricable. Even as they return to time, to the clutter of thought, they float together for another luscious, lingering moment.

When she is fully awake Agnes knows what is possible and wants to return and bring the girl with her again. The child belongs to her now, at last. They were together once and will be again, will recapture, or be captured by, that blissful intimacy. There is no sensation comparable, nothing as amazing as the infinity when two lives have blended.

But the girl seems so far away, blurry, hardly more substantial than a ghost. Only her eyes shine clearly, eyes as thickly red as the mind on a chloroform jag. Suddenly Agnes recognizes those eyes. Overcome, she clutches the handkerchief in her hand as she falls to her knees before the woman she has hidden from for twelve years. She tries to explain, to tell the woman how she'd lost so many mothers, so many babies, how that night she would have lost them both again, unable to do anything but watch the stormy transformation from birth into death. She is sorry for what she did. She is prepared if it happens again. And then there's the child to consider—doesn't it matter that she saved the life of the child?

The child! Agnes doesn't see her anywhere. She has disappeared into the woman, Agnes's victim and accuser. What are the words that will bring her back? What is her name? Agnes tells herself she will remember, she's determined to do it. Being determined doesn't help her much, though. It is as if the girl never existed, and Agnes, tricked by the illusive fumes of chloroform, has made a terrible mistake.

On the day Miss Agnes was expected back in town, the entire population of Tucksville, including the children, assembled at dawn outside the bank where the mail coach would let off its passengers and cargo. They had brought all the evidence they needed to confront the midwife: Father Cecil carried a burlap sack full of bones, the sheriff carried a basket full of bottles, and between them Myrtle stood like an angel framed by burning swords.

The coach was due to arrive at nine. A night mist still hung in the air. No one spoke. Only an occasional child broke the spell with a cough, and at one point a mongrel dog belonging to no one appeared from nowhere and began scratching at the cobblestones, until one man sent it howling with a kick.

The long wait was necessary, even intoxicating. With every minute that passed, the suspense grew more intense and the punishment to be exacted seemed more just. The citizens of Tucksville would do what they had to do, what Miss Agnes herself would expect them to do. There were no alternatives. *An eye for an eye* was the rule in such matters. Miss Agnes had taken Myrtle from her mother's womb without permission, and now the people of Tucksville were going to take the girl back.

DOROTHEA DIX:
SAMARITAN

*W*hen a girl was recalcitrant I used the whip, and if she didn't improve I would make her walk to and from school during Courthouse Week wearing a placard on her back stating "A Very Bad Girl Indeed." There is nothing more instructive than shame. I was only fourteen years old when I turned a vacant store in Worcester into a school. I lengthened my skirts and coiled my hair. More than once my handsome older cousin, Edward Bangs, invited me to a dance. Of course I declined. I was a young woman of neat and decorous habits. Besides, I had no time for amusements, not with thirty students dependent upon me for their education. I taught reading, writing, manners, and sewing. Later, at the school I started in the Dix family mansion in Boston, I broadened the curriculum to include astronomy, mineralogy, and natural sciences. Every evening I prepared the next day's lessons. I rarely went to sleep before midnight, and I was up by five A.M.

I've always been industrious, even as a small child. *Dolly, why don't you indulge yourself today?* my grandfather used to tease when I was little, tempting me with everything from chocolate-covered cherries to the sweet Dix pears that he had cultivated right in his own backyard. He was one to talk. Between his drugstore, his chemical factory, and his acres of farmland scattered throughout New England, he never rested. In my memory he is usually striding off, and I am running beside him, tugging at his trouser leg and begging him to take me along. My energy I inherited from my grandfather. My commitment comes from my father, a Methodist clergyman who rode around the state of Maine on horseback, saddlebags stuffed with tracts that my mother and I had bound with leather thread. He began to draw great crowds on the town greens, or so he reported to us. But he always returned empty-handed, and I would have to exchange the extra tracts for staples at the Hampden store.

It was there I came to know the meaning of shame and its disciplinary value. The women huddling together in the store would glance at me, and though I couldn't make out what they were whispering, from time to time I heard my father's name, *Joseph Dix*, rise up like a fish twisting from a stream. I could tell they pitied me and blamed my father for my condition. But I have always been wan and bony; in this respect I take after Mother. True, my father's temper combined with his strict sense of duty made him intolerant of my faults. I learned how to use the whip from him. And I learned how to survive with only the barest necessities. Having grown up in Dix Mansion, he had experienced luxury and renounced it. Our cabin was chinked with plaster, the floors were puncheon, and winter and summer alike we kept the small windows covered with oiled paper. All day long, day after day until I was twelve, I sat with my mother in front of the fireplace and pushed a needle through signatures of heavy printed paper.

I finally ran away to Boston, not to escape hardship or my father's punishments but to be as close to my grandfather as possible. He had been dead for five years by then, yet whenever I had visited I'd found him everywhere in Dix Mansion, in his books, in his pipe left out on his desk, in the fruit ripening in the garden. I was as devoted to the memory of Dr. Elijah Dix as much as I had been devoted to him in person—more as I grew older and could better appreciate his contributions.

My grandmother consented to take responsibility for my upbringing. My father forbade me from ever setting foot in his cabin in Hampden again. He died in April of 1821, when I was nineteen years old and had already devoted myself to a lifetime of service. I was still innocent, though. I would have to wait another twenty years before I saw the repulsive face of civilization beneath the mask. And even longer, to tell what I had seen.

This is the story of my life. Hopefully, you will learn from it. Perhaps a dozen lashes with the whip would help. If you still haven't taken my example to heart, you might try wearing a placard on your back.

Not that anyone should follow directly in my footsteps. You'd be hard pressed to find a girl of equal mettle. I was only twelve years old when I stole through the Maine woods one night and left my childhood behind forever. I knew I wouldn't have lasted much longer at home; if only I could have taken my mother with me. That she became an invalid early in life was no surprise. I doubt she could have made the journey even then, fifty miles on foot, nothing to eat for a week but a heel of bread and some cheese. I kept up my courage, though, just like Dick Whittington. The soles of my shoes were worn so thin that I could feel every pebble beneath my feet. I slept in barns, warmed by the heat of cattle. One night I curled on a bed of straw with a bitch and her brood of whining puppies. By the time I reached Dix Mansion five days after I'd set out, I was so caked with dirt that my grandmother's maid took me for a little beggar pick-aninny.

I don't think my grandmother welcomed my arrival. But she knew how her husband would have treated me if

he were alive. So for a two-year trial she kept me at Dix
Mansion, paid for tutors and dressed me in navy frocks
trimmed with lace. Finally she couldn't stand it any
longer. I was too impetuous, too willful, she said—
unjustly, in my opinion. I merely resented being treated
like a child. She sent me to Worcester to live with my
great-aunt and cousins, and there I was allowed to do
what came naturally: to teach. Since then I have never
missed an opportunity to crusade against ignorance. I
have been relentless. I don't consider it a coincidence that
my father's name was Joseph and my mother's name was
Mary.

I moved back to Dix Mansion after three years in
Worcester, in 1819, and made peace with my grandmother. It was she, not I, who had changed. In my
absence she came to realize that the independence she
had cursed me for was in fact a blessing. By then my
mother and brothers, neglected by my father, were desti-
tute, and I took it upon myself to support them. For this
reason alone my grandmother allowed me to start a
school at Dix Mansion. And she didn't protest when I
revealed my plans to open a charity school out in the
carriage house.

I'll tell you a little secret: I never punished a charity
girl with the placard. Not once.

The years passed. My cousin Edward asked me to
marry him and I refused. When I became ill with rheuma-

tism of the lungs, I had to close my schools. I recovered on a trip to St. Croix, where I visited a boiling house and saw a captured runaway slave wearing an iron collar around his neck. Back in Boston I wrote a pamphlet called "The Art of Introspection" for girls, which became very popular. I fell ill again and in 1837 went to Europe for a change of climate. I nearly died in a squalid hotel room near the docks in Liverpool and was nursed back to health by the gracious philanthropists Mr. and Mrs. William Rathbone of Greenbank. After spending a year pampered by them, I returned home to a legacy left to me by my grandmother, who had died the previous summer.

But it wasn't until I was thirty-nine years old that I finally found my purpose, thanks to Dr. Channing, minister of the Unitarian Church on Federal Street. Under his influence I had turned away from the Methodism of my father. Dr. Channing became a great friend—over the years I transcribed more than fifty of his sermons, and he often sought my opinion on church matters. It was an early-spring day in 1841 when he came to ask me if I could recommend a capable woman to lead a Bible class for female inmates at the East Cambridge jail, a request that would change my life.

I told him, "Sir, I know someone perfectly suited."

"Wonderful," he said, snapping shut the cover of his pocket watch after checking the time.

"If you have no objections, then, I'd like to offer myself."

Suddenly Dr. Channing was full of objections. He hadn't intended to solicit my services—he'd only wanted a recommendation and had in mind another sort of woman for the job, he protested. What sort? I inquired. He wouldn't answer me. But only after a great deal of argument did I manage to convince him that despite my gentility I was sufficiently stalwart to face an audience of prostitutes, thieves, and paupers.

I embarked upon my new program of reform the following Sunday. It become apparent that some formidable experience lay ahead, for as the coach crossed the Charles I had a vision, though not of the hallucinatory kind—there were no images other than the dismal reality of the muddy, swollen river, of my hands red and waxy from the cold, of the soot-colored sky. It was, I suppose, a premonition. The first time I heard the scream it began in my head. The next time, and from then on, it would come from without.

It was a woman's voice, hoarse from exertion, and instead of rising to a peak as most screams do, it tripped down an octave and turned into a moan. My own voice caught in my throat with a gulp, I was so startled. And even more than that, I was confused to find myself alone in the carriage, since for a moment the voice had conjured the presence of its owner so completely that I felt warm breath against my cheek. Inspired by fear and ending in despair, it was a sound that would become appallingly familiar. Whenever I heard it I knew there were radical changes to be made, if not by persuasion, then by force. The whip and the placard. With such firm methods I have achieved my ends. Some people consider me a moral autocrat.

Dolly, why don't you let it alone for an hour or two? my grandfather used to say when I was concentrating hard on my alphabet book on a Sunday afternoon. Then he'd bundle me in an afghan and sneak me out to the carriage house, and we'd spend the rest of the day driving around the city, past his drugstore beside Faneuil Hall, through South Boston to the chemical factory. It was Dr. Elijah Dix who showed me what one person can do if he sets his mind to it. We are remembered through our work. And in case people forget my contribution after I am gone, they can refer to this memoir. Here is the epigraph I would like to use:

> *Drink freely and bestow*
> *A kindly thought on her*
> *Who bade this fountain flow.*

These words were written for me by the poet John Whittier and engraved on a fountain I donated for thirsty animals in the Boston Commons. For more than forty years I have been the representative for the dumb, man and beast alike. All I ask now is that the lesson of my life be memorized by others. The fountain must never stop flowing and the asylums must never be shut down.

Dolly, why don't you let it alone? I confess this is exactly what I was thinking after I'd finished reading the story of Mary Magdalene to the inmates of the East Cambridge jail and was following the jailer down the corridor to the cell for the insane. I'd heard a woman screaming and demanded to be escorted to her. At first the jailer hesitated, likely because he was embarrassed by the degree of neglect—he maintained that it was "no sight for a lady" and that I "shouldn't mind about that." I faced him squarely and told him, "Sir, I insist," though secretly I wanted to leave that fulsome place. But my duty was becoming apparent to me even then, and when the jailer saw that I wouldn't back down, he relented with a shrug.

We came to a barred door—the first of many barred doors that have temporarily blocked my way. Silence on the other side made it more difficult to imagine what I would find. Then I heard the scream again. From this sound, nearly identical to the scream I had heard as I crossed the Charles, I knew exactly what was waiting behind the door as clearly as if it had been myself locked inside. Or I thought I knew.

"There's no keeping them quiet," the jailer said as he lifted the bar.

Them. In the second before the door was opened I doubled my expectations. The woman I assumed I'd find, the woman who was a version of myself, what I would have been had I remained at my mother's side in the Hampden cottage sewing tracts all day, was *two* women. I saw both of them in my mind for an instant before I saw them in person locked in separate pens made of rough pine boards. The older woman was naked, pulling at the slats of her cage; long hair the color of dirty snow fell to her waist. When she saw us she screamed again. The younger woman squatted in the rear of her cage, a blanket wrapped around her legs and a second blanket draped over her shoulders and head in a cowl fashion. Two women. Two blankets. Why did the younger woman have two blankets and the older woman none at all? This was my immediate question, though I didn't ask it. Instead I asked the jailer why these women had no stove to warm them.

"Because they'd set themselves on fire," he explained.

But I understood them better than that. I knew how far they'd go. And when they'd stop. I knew there wasn't any danger in a stove. The most important nutrient for the human spirit is warmth, the next, freedom. These two women hadn't committed any sin, no more than a bluejay in the trees sins when he squawks, and they deserved to be treated with compassion.

The eyes of the younger woman were lusterless in the

light cast by the jailer's lantern, yet I found the wild, rolling eyes of the older woman more distressing. She would be difficult to save. It was my duty to save her. Them. Both of them. All of them. My mission suddenly became clear, and I felt the urgency of time as never before, the future pressing in, cruelties repeating themselves like reflections in opposing mirrors—unless I interfered.

When the woman thrust her chin through the slats and screamed for the third time, I saw the cloud her breath made in the cold prison air. Why did the younger woman have two blankets and the older woman none at all? Why couldn't I bring myself to ask the jailer this?

"There's no keeping them quiet," he said again.

I set my Bible on the floor of the younger woman's pen. I didn't try to speak either to her or to the maniac. Surely they both understood that I would help—recognition was too strong for them not to sense it.

And so I surrendered to my convictions. When I was twelve I'd given up my childhood. At the age of thirty-nine I gave up my womanhood to the cause of the pauper insane. I began by reading histories at the Boston Athenaeum: of London's Bedlam, where jailers charged the general public an admission of one penny to see the most violent inmates; of La Salpêtrière in the sewers in Paris, where madwomen were chained to the walls and slowly gnawed to death by rats; of my own Commonwealth of

Massachusetts, where until 1827 the insane were committed to prison for their entire lives. Then I took to the countryside of New England. Before I was through I'd covered eight thousand miles by train, by stagecoach and carriage, by foot. I became a well-known sight in my dark dress and white kerchiefs, too often an unwelcome sight. "There are some, and Miss Dix may be one of them, who are always on tiptoe, looking for something more marvelous than is to be discovered in real life," wrote one venomous reporter, suggesting that the horrors I'd witnessed had been conjured in my own imagination. But I am not inventive enough to fill a single page with such vivid fancy, much less the entire volume of facts and statistics, which I presented to the Legislature of Massachusetts in 1843. "I tell what I have seen—painful and shocking as the details are." This was my pledge from the beginning. I am too plain to be a liar, too full of common sense. I described what I'd seen in the shacks and cellars and almshouses of the region. At first the lawmakers were resistant to my message, but the truth proved too powerful, and I finally steered them in favor of reform.

Beyond the law, though, lies the obstacle of public prejudice. My influence in this respect is far diminished, now that I am restricted to bed and am too weak to snap a whip.

Although I am an invalid, when I am neither writing, receiving visitors, nor sleeping I often think about my good fortune and the difference between what I have and what is possible. I have a soapstone wrapped in wool to keep my feet warm. I have nurses and doctors to monitor my health. I have as many blankets as I need. I am not kept in a closet below a staircase, in the cellar of a poorhouse, in an unheated shanty eight by ten feet square. I am not filthy and do not feel compelled to tear off my own skin with my fingernails. I have not lost my limbs to frostbite and gangrene. The truth is best summed up in the familiar phrase *there but for the grace of God*.

There: in a foul pen in the East Cambridge jail. There: hidden from the rest of humanity because she never mastered any useful skill, and being untrained and without financial support after both her parents succumbed to tuberculosis, she was forced into the street to beg for bread, and being a girl, it wasn't long before men began to take advantage of her hunger. How could she have protected herself? They took what they wanted until there was nothing but a little bit of flesh and bone left, no soul, no hope, no intelligence. Then they locked her in prison and soon she had permanent welts on her face from pressing up against the slats. Without a window she lost track of time. Sometimes the lamp on the wall was lit, sometimes it wasn't, she never knew why, nor did she know who the other woman was they put in the room with her, a young whelp of a thing who never spoke. She couldn't stand the quiet and the *plock plock plock* of water dripping from a pipe onto the cement floor, so she screamed to get a rise from her companion. Nothing worked. No one came to see what was the matter or to wash her dress, which grew so foul that it made her itch, so she ripped it to shreds. When winter came they brought her an old blanket smelling of manure. What happened to that blanket? It vanished, that's what happened. It simply vanished. And they never gave her another.

The poor maniac of the East Cambridge Prison for Women could tell me about everything else, but she couldn't tell me how she'd lost the blanket, though I asked her countless times. Did she pass it through the bars to the younger woman? Did the younger woman steal it from her during the night?

I don't know why the question of the blanket should continue to distract me so: the maniac is long since dead, and the younger woman was advertised and taken in as a servant by a gentleman farmer and his wife. They have treated her kindly, I've made sure of it.

But though the two women in the East Cambridge jail were the inspiration, my ambition immediately became much larger. I wanted to do more than correct the evils I had seen; I wanted to make sure that ignorance wouldn't perpetuate itself. So I not only attacked the existing laws but raised money to build asylums. I found hundreds of forgotten souls wasting away in darkness; without exception their eyes were black and slow to respond to light, their clothes were ragged, their hair was so populated with lice we were forced to shave their heads. I found them in darkness and brought them into rooms awash in brilliant white light. Every room in every asylum I have opened has clean white walls and at least one window. There are two windows here in "The Royal Suite," as the attendants have called it since I took up residence. I tried to insist that I could do very well in an ordinary room, but the director wouldn't listen. Dorothea Dix must be treated like a queen, he said. So I've tolerated my privileges, but only to humor him. This Trenton asylum was my first notable accomplishment, and I love it as dearly as a firstborn child. If they put me in the boiler room with a collar around my neck, I wouldn't mind, as long as I knew that my work was being continued above.

But here I am surrounded by all this finery of white and glass, and here I receive my visitors; doctors from all over the world come to ask my advice, on New Year's Day my cousin Edward Bangs visits with his three darling granddaughters, and occasionally neatly dressed strangers, formerly insane, now independent, come to thank me. They are my life's justification.

My favorite visitor, however, is the East Cambridge maniac. She appears late at night when everyone else is asleep. Covered only by her long hair, she sits on the end of the bed without lighting the lamp—she is the one soul I couldn't save from darkness. Before I could have her transferred here to the Trenton asylum, she was dead. Now she is as shy of light as she is of people.

I know she is dead—I may be an invalid but I am not confused. I also know that she comes from the outside. She is not a hallucination, no more than she was when I first saw her. We have a lot in common, she and I. *There but for the grace of God.* I have apologized more than once for not rescuing her, but she always waves away my words impatiently.

She tells me the story of her life in hopes that I will learn from her example. A forgotten life is a meaningless life, she says. We agree about so many things. She is the reason I have begun drafting this memoir—not for her but because of her. *Remember me,* she whispers every night before she leaves, bending so close that her lips brush against my cheek.

Remember me.

I wish she could tell me what happened to that blanket. I've offered to give her one of mine, but she always refuses. I don't think she can distinguish between hot and cold anymore. Or maybe it's just that her experiences have left her indifferent.

I know she is not a product of my imagination because she is not followed by others I'd like to see again—my grandfather, for instance. *Dolly, why don't you get dressed and come along with me?* he'd say, forever tempting. And maybe I would go with him, run away from my beloved firstborn child, the Trenton State Asylum, as I once ran away from my mother and father.

I wouldn't mind seeing my parents again. Rather, I'd like to be seen by them, especially by my father, to prove to him that I didn't come to a bad end. Like him, I have sacrificed everything to my mission. But here the similarity ends. My father's influence was intangible, or even worse, insignificant. He would tell my mother and me about spoiled young girls who threw off their earrings and farmers who fell to their knees and wept when he preached. But he recounted these same conversions over and over, and in my opinion he enjoyed boasting more than preaching. My influence, in contrast, is visible not only in the people I've saved but in the one hundred and twenty-three asylums and hospitals that have sheltered them. How slowly it happened—brick by brick by brick over forty years—but these sanctuaries will stand long after I have disappeared, and my work will be carried on without me.

I suppose *she* will continue haunting this asylum even when I'm no longer present to receive her. She won't be able to rest until she is treated justly, which won't happen, I assume, until time ends. Surprisingly, she holds no grudges. Her only regret is that she never fell in love, though early in her life she had the opportunity. If only she had returned the love of the one man who had loved her; instead she despised him for being nothing but a dairy hand and sent him away, unable to foresee the turn of events—her parents' illnesses, her own rapid deterioration. She might have spent her life tugging on cow udders and churning butter and bearing children, not happily married, perhaps, but well-fed and secure.

I try to reassure her. Few women could match her for stamina, I say. So what if she lost her mind? She should be proud of her ability to survive. When I say this she shakes her head and frowns, but I suspect she likes to hear it. The account of her life is meaningful only insofar as she has been self-sufficient. This might be why I found her in her cage without a blanket—perhaps she cast it aside to prove that she didn't need anything from anyone.

I would like to think I have been as self-sufficient as the maniac and have managed by a more powerful strength of will to avoid her fate. *There but for the grace of God.* But I have to thank the grace of my wealthy grandparents as well. Money is one antidote to madness; charity is another. I accepted the former and paid for my advantages with the latter. The maniac accepted neither. Her last years were as grim and solitary as mine will be full of admirers and light. When she talks about that period of her life and the single desire to escape that filled her consciousness, her voice starts to quaver, as though simply the memory were enough to induce the screams.

If she screams the nurses will come running, someone

will fetch the director, and I'll have plenty of explaining to do. So I am always hasty to remind her that we are both exceptional women, in different ways.

Dolly, I always knew you'd make me proud, Grandfather Dix would say if he were sitting on the end of my bed in the maniac's place. He was the only one in the family who sensed my potential. But I imagine even he'd be surprised when I told him about the second half of my life, how after finishing my work in New England I carried my message to France, Italy, Turkey, and Palestine, how throughout the world strangers gathered to wish me *bon voyage* and to kiss the hem of my dress, how I once had an audience with Pope Pius IX, who gave me his entire consideration.

I wish my grandfather would visit. I admit: what I wanted most was to impress him. Instead, I am left trying to make an impression upon you, my reader, whom I'll never meet. Maybe you haven't even been born yet and I don't exist anymore. No matter how exceptional we are, we vanish. I don't like to think about how in a few years Dorothea Dix will be just another old-fashioned female samaritan from the past, and in a few more years she'll be forgotten. Who will care?

When the maniac talks I am as rapt an audience as I was when Dr. Channing delivered his sermons. The longer she stays in my room, the more she dwells upon that final portion of her life when every day repeated the previous day without variation and she wanted only to be outside her cage and could do nothing but scream, until the scream became the purpose. Unable to recall what she was screaming for, she screamed in echo of herself.

When she tells me this, I see the corners of her lips twitching. Her hysteria would be contagious. I dread the scene. What would I say to the director? The maniac is not just another patient—she is my shadow, the emblem of my failure. When I first looked upon her and her companion in the East Cambridge prison, I saw my own future, a future that I'd been spared. Or so I thought. I've come to realize that she and I are converging—we've left the dull-eyed younger woman behind and are coming closer and closer together, like the earth's shadow and the moon during an eclipse. *There but for the grace of God*, I remind myself. If only I could contain my fascination. But I must listen until she has nothing more to tell. This is my one remaining duty: to follow her story to the end.

Poor Dolly, you've had your own trials, haven't you?

I certainly have, Grandfather. I know what it's like to be cold all the time and locked away like Gretel deep in the witch's forest. I was my father's prisoner through my childhood, I slept on the floor in the attic, I never had enough to eat and would have gone mad if it hadn't been for you, Grandfather, and our holidays together. Twice a year you brought me to Boston, and there you showed me what was possible.

He showed me, I mean. I am not confused. He died

when I was only seven, and I am still alive, alone in the Royal Suite overlooking the Greek portico at the Trenton State Asylum. It is after midnight, and my favorite visitor hasn't yet arrived. I can still feel her icy fingers cupped around my hands as she said good-bye to me last night. She has almost reached the conclusion of her story. When she finishes, it will be my turn to talk and hers to listen. But at the rate she's going she'll never finish, at least not in my lifetime. Her account has begun to wander as wildly as her mind did during her final hour when every past experience took on a new immediacy, distracting her, mixing up the little bit of sense she had left. Near the end she didn't know who or where she was, though she could recall herself as a little girl with unexpected accuracy, strolling along a garden path, hand in hand with her father. When she saw a baby sparrow hopping in circles on the slate, she wanted to return it to its nest, but her father told her she mustn't touch it, explaining that a mother will abandon a fledgling that smells of human hands. And he pulled her away.

Strange as it may sound, when she recounted this sentimental anecdote I started to weep; the stoical, tireless Dorothea Dix bawled like an infant, though not because she felt sorry for the maniac. Rather, she felt sorry for herself since, coincidentally, she'd had a similar experience as a young child: the man had been her grandfather and the garden had been the one enclosed by brick walls behind the Dix family mansion, and she was only five years old.

I was only five years old, I mean. I am Dorothea Dix, moral autocrat and international samaritan, and I will soon be gone. Death is just another poorly mapped land that I must visit, like the state of Texas. I traveled to Texas by myself in 1856, hoping to secure large grants of prairie to use for my asylums. This was after I'd been abroad but before the war, before I was appointed Head Supervisor for Military Hospitals, and my fame still hadn't reached into the West. So you can imagine my surprise when I had finished eating dinner at a roadhouse and took out my purse to pay and the owner said to me, "No thank you, Miss Dix, I don't take money from you, who have been good to everybody for years and years."

Dorothea Dix was good to everybody for years and years. Dorothea Dix was one of the most useful and distinguished women America has ever produced. This is what my friend, the poet John Whittier, will write in his eulogy for me after I am dead, though others will find less favorable adjectives—"queer and arbitrary," as Louisa May Alcott described me after I personally nursed her through typhoid at the Georgetown Military Hospital. "She is a kind old soul, but very queer and arbitrary" is the exact quote, according to the gossip. Not that I pay any attention to gossip, except the most revealing kind. Generally I find the chatter of women tiresome. Which is why in my advertisement for military nurses I stated: "No woman under thirty need apply. All nurses required to be plain-looking women. Their dresses must be black or brown, with no bows, no curls, no jewelry, and no hoop skirts." The more frills donned by a young woman, the smaller her contribution. Give me a homely old maid and I will turn her experiences to great advantage.

Give me the maniac. There is no one plainer, no one more experienced. And I don't say this to flatter her.

She will be here soon. First I will ask her to fetch me a glass of water and another pillow, then she can pick up where she left off. If I'm not confused, last night she told the sad little tale about the sparrow, one of life's hard lessons, how well I know. I would have gone mad like her were it not for my grandfather, who taught me about the satisfaction of work. Perhaps the maniac screamed to keep busy. Good Lord, it was something to do, a way to fill the void. I wonder what it's like to have absolutely nothing, not even a blanket to keep her warm and respectable. I wonder what happened to the blanket, why she gave it up, thrusting it through the slats of her pen toward the younger woman, who stared blankly. If there were a stove in the room, the maniac would have burned the blanket in spite, reduced it to ashes, and though the jailer would have said, "I told you so," she would have laughed aloud. That's what I would have done, laughed at that stupid young woman for missing an opportunity. But there was no stove, and somehow the blanket was successfully passed from the maniac to her prison mate, maybe with the jailer's help, maybe at his insistence. Yes, in all probability the jailer was the force behind the transaction. I understand now: the jailer was an ordinary man with ordinary tastes and preferred the downy chick to the hag. How well I understand. Too well. So as it turns out it's not a story she needs to share, since it's a familiar story, as old as Adam, the story of the blanket. It makes me so angry I could tear off my nightgown—the one embroidered by Sylvia, the wife of my cousin Edward Bangs—I could scream like the maniac.

She'll be here any minute. I will tell her that I'm not confused anymore, I understand everything. She'd better hurry. If I scream the nurses will fetch the director and I'll have plenty of explaining to do. What will happen to my reputation? I won't scream, it's too risky. I am and will remain Dorothea Dix, America's most useful and distinguished woman. I have a soapstone to keep my feet warm and as many blankets as I need, as many as I could ever want.

X NUMBER
OF POSSIBILITIES

*T*heodore von Grift lives a counterfeit life neither out of habit nor choice but out of self-defense. His tastes have been carefully acquired. Soft-boiled eggs, steak tartare, the fragrance of peonies, lawn tennis: the list has nothing genuine about it, since appreciation for Theodore von Grift is only an act. He abandoned his authentic self so long ago that he wouldn't recognize him if they met on a street in downtown Baltimore. That he lives at number fifty-five Penrose Street in Baltimore, Maryland, is as unnatural as any other aspect of his life. His position as a bank officer, his wife and two children, his four-bedroom house—all contribute to the elaborate composition. He is not who he is and doesn't try to resolve the paradox. Instead, he fills in the role he originated, each day adds new details, and by 1927 has grown so intricate, so complex, that the many people who early on recognized his personality as a mask have dwindled to one.

Theodore is being revealed, investigated, stripped, and examined by a mere child. He doesn't even know the boy's name, nor have they ever spoken. But every morning the boy is sitting on the porch steps of number sixty-three when Theodore walks by on his way to the trolley stop on Fulton Avenue. Sixty-three is the most dilapidated house on the block, the shingles sloughing, the shutters hanging crookedly, and ordinarily Theodore would have ignored these neighbors. But there is something about the way the boy looks up from the scab on his knee and stares: a wise, unnerving stare, as though he can see beneath Theodore's clothes. Theodore has spent half his lifetime protecting himself from observation, has perfected impenetrability and is to acquaintances and family what lead is to the X ray. And now, in his forty-ninth year, he has met his match in an unkempt little boy.

He could easily take a roundabout route and avoid the child. But the challenge is too compelling: he walks by number sixty-three in order to test himself, and though he continues to fail the test, he has not given in to discouragement. If one sheet of lead doesn't shield him from those prying eyes, he will try two; if two don't suffice, he will try platinum. Eventually he will be to the child what he is to everyone else—only surface—and the boy will forget what he has seen. Young children have short, selective memories. There will be enough distractions in his life, and Theodore von Grift will fade with most of the boy's past, just as he has faded from himself.

"I should remember," Wilhelm Conrad Röntgen, inventor of the X ray, once wrote to a friend, "where there is much light there is also much shadow." Theodore's adult life remains clear in his memory, but the years of his childhood are hidden in shadow. It is not *as if* he died on or around his eighteenth birthday. The figurative expression is nearly literal in his case, a case notable enough to be written up in *Scientific American*, earning him invitations to lecture at two German universities. But because the fame of the case was inspired by the new Röntgen rays rather than by his remarkable recovery, and, more important, because he had to reconstruct his personality from scratch, he had declined the invitations, booked a passage to the United States, and under a pseudonym (now his permanent name, thirty-one years later) began life over again.

He remembers the first days of adulthood only through a few stark impressions: the face of an old woman, her crooked teeth which looked as soft as hot tallow. A man, presumably his doctor, breathing stale tobacco as he peered into his ear. And nuns, dozens of nuns bustling about the room—like gray rats, Theodore had thought as he sleepily watched them from his bed.

He had been living in Munich; where he'd come from

he didn't know. The doctor could tell him only this: that he'd been found lying in a park, his hair matted with blood, his fingers still tangled around the trigger of a pistol. No identification was found. He'd been transported to a nearby hospital. A surgeon neatly sutured the wound after deciding that the bullet was too deeply embedded to be removed, and Theodore remained an invalid at the hospital for five months.

The hospital nuns called him Anton because he often murmured the name in his sleep. They grew fond of him, intrigued, perhaps, by his amnesia, and when he was strong enough to leave, they gave him a wallet full of money to maintain him until he could find work. They offered to love him like a son if he couldn't locate his own parents, told him to consider the hospital his permanent home. But life on the busy city streets absorbed him as soon as he walked out into daylight, and he left the hospital behind forever.

While he had been convalescing, the police had made inquiries and advertised in newspapers for any information concerning the young man known as Anton, age approximately eighteen. But no one had come forward. He must have been a stranger in Munich, without friends or relatives in the city. And Theodore, then Anton, found himself increasingly grateful for the mystery of his past. Whatever he'd been in his previous life, he'd been driven to suicide. So it was best to forget that life, along with the nuns, the hospital, the bullet in his head. The German language and an impressive mathematical ability were the only souvenirs from his youth. At the age of eighteen (approximately), he had thirty crowns to his name, whatever name he chose. Even as he'd boarded a train for Hamburg the day he was released from the hospital, he gave himself a new name, Hermann, as though this were enough to dismiss the former self entirely, the self hidden just beyond the boundary of his awareness.

Can the child sitting on the steps of number sixty-three Penrose Street in Baltimore see what Theodore can't see? The secrets of his past, which are to Theodore no more than countless possibilities? He is like a pocket watch and the boy does what most children will do if given the chance. He smashes the watch so he can investigate its parts. Smashes Theodore every time he walks by. Twirls his dirty little forefinger in his cowlick and stares at Theodore with smug innocence, which makes the man, by contrast, guilty.

What have I done? Theodore has been wondering since the boy first stationed himself on the steps last August. His first memory is of the old woman's teeth. Before that, his recollections are all speculative. He imagines himself sprawled on the ground, spread-eagle, blood crusted on his brow. Is this what the little boy sees? Or worse? And what came before? What crime did Theodore commit that drove him to the crime of suicide?

Try this, he tells himself repeatedly. *Make your mind blank. White.* Beyond the oranges and reds of Baltimore row houses he sees white walls, four windowless walls as white as paper. Anton, Hermann, Theodore. Anton's eyes were covered with white bandages. Hermann was surrounded by whitewashed walls. Theodore's mind is nearly blank, dominated by these memories of blankness, and what he wants is identical to what he wanted: to escape. His was a wild animal's rage. As Hermann he had leaped at a man, gripped his throat, throttled him, all the while blinded by the intensity of white. *This is what I will do to you, boy,* Theodore von Grift thinks, flexing his fingers as he walks on. *Don't touch me. They called me mad once. Come too close and you won't live to tell what happened.*

It is the same sequence every morning, and by the time Theodore has reached State Street, his face shines with perspiration, his chest heaves, the design of his life has begun to unravel.

In truth, he was never mad, or at least no more mad than a man strung on the rack. He had a bullet in his head, and Theodore—rather, Hermann—believed that if the bullet were removed he would regain control over himself. But he was living in Hamburg by then, and he couldn't recall the name of the hospital where he'd been treated. He could only point to the side of his head and insist repeatedly, "Here, I shot myself here." The Hamburg doctors, seeing no sign of a scar, labeled him insane.

The fault was his. Without references or personal history—before he'd invented a story for himself—he'd been unable to find a job, so in the beginning he'd done nothing but wander the streets, spending his money on coffee, bread, and rent. Soon the headaches began, and after three months, when the pain grew too intense to bear, he'd gone to a doctor and asked him to remove the bullet. The doctor asked for a detailed account, so Theodore explained how at the age of eighteen he had tried to kill himself.

It was in the doctor's office where Theodore first lost control. In the middle of his visit, without provocation, he suddenly seized the doctor by his neck, nearly strangling him to death. He attacked the policemen who came to carry him off to jail. He fought with the attendants transporting him to the asylum. He even sprang at a nurse, a young woman who, with astonishing strength, subdued him with a punch that split his lower lip. Not until the director informed him that he'd been committed to the Hamburg asylum did he realize what he'd done.

I have a bullet embedded in my head. I am not mad; the bullet makes me crazy, blinds me, all I can see is the white light of my pain. I want to stop the pain, nothing else. Don't blame me—blame the bullet in my head. You think these are a lunatic's ravings. Cut me open, see for yourself. I don't remember who I was, how I survived. I know I shot myself. I can't explain why there is no scar. The nuns, ask the nuns. I don't remember where they were, but they must be somewhere still. Let me out and I'll find them. They'll assure you that I'm speaking the truth. My name is Hermann Glasser. I give you my permission to operate. I implore you. Go ahead—for curiosity's sake, then, if for no other reason. I want to live a normal life, work hard all week and on Sundays shoot woodcocks from the window of a little bird-branch hut. But I cannot acquire a hunting license as long as I am legally insane. Help me.

For ten years he had raged, begged, wept, but the doctors remained unmoved. In their informed opinion everything he said was governed by the skewed logic of his main delusion: the patient named Hermann believed he had a bullet in his head. After extensive examination the doctors proclaimed him incurable, and he became just another inmate of the asylum, another child-man to hide from his easily disgusted fellow Germans.

Against all odds he had survived, emerged from the asylum at the age of twenty-nine—approximately—not only sane but famous enough to share a page in *Scientific American* with an English swallow. The swallow's feat was to fly from London to its nest on a Shropshire farm at a speed of two miles per minute. Theodore's feat was to be among the first to demonstrate the usefulness of the recently discovered X ray.

"A Hamburg young man has just had his sanity proved by the Roentgen rays. He declared ten years ago that he had a bullet in his head which he had fired into it in trying to commit suicide. He complained of pain, and as he attacked his keepers and the doctors could find no trace of the wound, was locked up as a dangerous lunatic. The Roentgen rays have now shown the exact place of the bullet." *Scientific American*, November 7, 1896.

This is the only true story of his life. Thirty-one years later Theodore von Grift, the former phenomenon, is an average man weighing one hundred and forty pounds and composed of enough water to fill a ten-gallon barrel, enough fat for seven cakes of soap, enough carbon for nine thousand lead pencils, enough phosphorus to make twenty-two hundred match heads, sufficient magnesium for one dose of salts, enough iron to make one medium-sized nail, sufficient lime to whitewash a chicken coop, and enough sulfur to rid one dog of fleas. An average man who is an average combination of nutrients and poisons. What more is there to know?

Ask the boy.

But Theodore has seen into his own head; he doesn't want to see any more. The bullet was removed over three decades ago, and the only pain he felt for years, before the boy at number sixty-three began to haunt him, was the occasional late-afternoon stab of hunger. Typical pain. Eight hours a day he has devoted himself to balancing the debit and credit columns. He eats lunch at Estes Grill with three or four colleagues, always ordering the same chowder and the same beer. He leaves work at six, buys the evening paper, and walks to the trolley station alone.

The porch steps of number sixty-three are empty in the evening, the house as unconcerned as a drunk sleeping on the street. His own home, number fifty-five, is always tidy on the outside and bustling inside, his ten-year-old son flying paper airplanes in the living room, his eight-year-old daughter screaming at her mother because she doesn't like onions, her mother knows she doesn't like onions yet still she puts chopped onions in the meatloaf.

You shouldn't speak to your mother that way.

Always the same routine, which is just how Theodore von Grift wants it, with occasional delicacies to relieve the tedium and distinguish him from the lower classes. Soft-boiled eggs, steak tartare . . . He is a naturalized American now. His wife knows the few facts of her husband's life and is content with the mystery of his youth, perhaps even intrigued by it, like the nuns had been. Easily satisfied, she fills her days with household chores and as a hobby raises African violets. Nothing makes her prouder than a blue ribbon in the annual garden competition. His son wants to be a fighter pilot; his daughter wants to grow her hair to her ankles.

What more is there to know? Or tell? Theodore's story begins and ends in a single paragraph in the November 7, 1896, issue of *Scientific American*. He has served his purpose and wants to be left alone. And whatever happens, whatever other injuries he sustains, he will never submit to an X ray again. He hadn't anticipated the consequences or even understood at the time what an X ray meant. X stood for unknown character. Because of the X ray—he'd had thirty-two X rays taken before the doctors had finished with him—the bullet had been located and removed, and he no longer explodes in violent rages. But in recent months, ever since the impertinent boy assumed his place on the front steps of sixty-three Penrose, Theodore has rarely enjoyed a full night's rest. In the early-morning hours he is awakened by the same panic that he feels when he walks past the boy.

The dream recurs, with minor variations: he is herded with a group of people, about two dozen in all, into a large examination room. A doctor directs the group to chairs arranged opposite the long, tubular lens of an X-ray machine. The doctor turns the machine on, aims the lens, and after a few seconds—just long enough for him to reach the exit—hot light washes over the rows of patients.

What unnerves Theodore in the dream is the doctor's hasty retreat. Why must he leave the room when he turns on the machine? Theodore will puzzle over this, his confusion will escalate under the heat of the X ray, and he will have to grip the seat of his chair in order to keep himself steady. Panic wakes him and keeps him awake for an hour or more, and the light that fills his mind during this time is not the familiar light of pain but of unspeakable fear.

In 1927, Theodore's forty-ninth year, most scientists believe that light is only beneficial: light cures rickets in young children, protects against scurvy, regulates the absorption and metabolism of calcium, prevents pellagra in man and black tongue in animals. Light is necessary to life, and the X ray, thirty-two years after its discovery, is essential to medical diagnosis. Decades will pass before opinions change and the dangers of light, even life-sustaining sunlight, are identified. So why does Theodore feel that he has been poisoned? Theodore has thirty-two X rays inside his head. All it takes is a single able interpreter to see what the light exposes: the first eighteen years of his life, eighteen years of secrets.

It is the middle of December, ten days before Christmas, when Theodore finally decides to confront the boy at number sixty-three. He passes a restless night; awakened at three A.M. by his dream, he lies awake until dawn imagining various retaliations against the boy. His visions disgust and delight him. Since the bullet had been removed, he has steadily gained self-control and rarely even engages in an argument. He knows he could never harm an innocent child. But it is this very innocence that gives the boy his power, Theodore believes. The child sees what the light exposes. Theodore must be reasonable;

instead of confronting the boy he will befriend him. He will convince the boy that he, Theodore von Grift, is hiding nothing. Children are gullible. In the name of self-defense Theodore will take advantage of the boy's trusting nature.

After a breakfast of toast—the crust slightly burnt, just the way he likes it—rich black coffee, and a soft-boiled egg in a silver-plated egg cup, he props his hat at a thirty-degree tilt from left to right, winds his pocket watch, and sets off: a thoroughly average man on an average day. His breath frosts in the winter air. He feels both uneasy and capable—his enemy is only a child, after all. But wouldn't it be easier if the child were an adult, Theodore's equal? He's not sure how he will open the conversation, decides too late that he should have brought some candy to use as bait.

The boy is there, sitting on the second step of number sixty-three, pulling at a loose thread hanging from the cuff of his plaid jacket. He turns up his face at the tap of Theodore's footsteps on the sidewalk, and his eyes settle into that offensive stare.

Hello there, Theodore intends to begin. But the conversation needs direction. *Hello there, young man, fine day today.* No, this won't do at all—it is too stiff, too mature. *And how are you this morning?* Too intimate for a child. *Hello there. Tell me, shouldn't someone be looking after you?* Too accusatory. Try this: *Hello there, early riser.*

"Hello there, early riser."

"Hello."

Just then Theodore sees a woman cross behind the front window, and he hurries on, all too aware of the hint of impropriety in his address to the boy. There is more than neighborly cheer in his intentions. But what, exactly, does he intend? He still isn't certain, though he imagines that the boy's mother would not approve. As he rounds the corner, he grinds his fist into his open hand, furious at his stupidity. The child is not alone in the world—he'd forgotten this. If he's going to make a companion of the boy, he'll have to contend with the mother. Or befriend the mother first. Now here's an idea: seduce the mother, and the boy will follow. Theodore has no interest in other women, though. His wife fits perfectly into his life, and he knows better than to take a risk that might lead to ruin. All he really needs to do is to convince the mother that he wants to help.

Help me.

To help himself—like a glutton at the dinner table, pleasure-seeker that he is, or so she might conclude and warn her boy away from him. That won't do. It's best to avoid the mother and go straight to the child. He shouldn't have hurried away so quickly this morning. The mother probably hadn't even noticed him.

By the time he arrives at his office building, he has decided to be honest with the boy, the most difficult approach, since his honesty is rooted in an intricate deception. He is not who he is. If the boy sees this, then surely he will see Theodore's true motives.

Stop looking at me. This is what he wants to tell the boy. But how to work his way toward the command? It is a difficult task, far more difficult than subtracting expenditures from income, so Theodore can fulfill his duties at the office even while his mind wanders and he contemplates various approaches to the dangerous little gorgon at number sixty-three.

By this point in the year Sacco and Vanzetti are dead, Trotsky has been expelled from the Communist party, the German economic system has collapsed, and Lindbergh has landed the *Spirit of St. Louis* in Paris. These are the subjects of lunchtime conversation, but today Theodore skips lunch, for he wants to be alone. He walks with shoulders hunched along Patapsco Street wishing he were entirely invisible. Because of the X rays inside him his bones show through his transparent skin. No one notices except the boy. Theodore feels him watching from every downtown window.

He pauses in front of a toy shop, locks himself in place, and faces the display as though it were the child. *We'll see who falters first.* He is looking at a Christmas scene: wooden elves at work, Santa bulging like a ripe red bud from a chimney, reindeer on the roof, cotton snow on the ground, a wooden locomotive stalled on wooden tracks, its tiny conductor standing inside, gazing at the world. Christmas in Toyland, and Theodore's thoughts grind to a halt, as though he himself has changed from flesh to wood, transformed into a toy himself. He has been struck by an idea, a masterful idea, and he feels safer than he's felt in years. He sees his answer here in the conductor's eyes, painted beads no bigger than pinheads. How long has it been since he understood an image so completely, in its full meaning and potential?

He leaves work half an hour early that evening. Wouldn't it be wonderful if the streets were covered with cotton snow and reindeer were pulling the jalopies? There is no snow in Baltimore. Still, that doesn't mean a man can't celebrate tradition. In front of number sixty-three Theodore tucks the package inside his coat and clumps loudly up the warped porch steps. The woman has opened the door before he's had a chance to knock. Theodore is not afraid. He removes his hat and asks to see her little boy. He notices that she looks too elderly to be the mother of such a young child. Perhaps she is his grandmother. With gray hair in a bun pulled so tight that it seems to stretch the wrinkles of her forehead into broad dents, she squints at Theodore, arms folded, and clears her throat as if to speak. Then she changes her mind and disappears, leaving the door open. Theodore steps into the front hallway. The house is rank with the smells of cooking fat, kerosene, stale wine. In a moment the woman returns, pushing the boy ahead of her. Perhaps she thinks that Theodore is a benefactor; she wouldn't be far from the truth.

Now Theodore may study the boy up close. The child has a plump, round face that looks so young Theodore is almost surprised to see teeth when the boy smiles. He must be five years old, at least, but there is something oddly infantile about him, and with his aged guardian behind, the pair seems laughably anachronistic. She stands with her arms folded, waiting.

"Hello there, early riser."

Theodore and the boy grin at each other like distrustful competitors. For the first time Theodore can meet the assault with impervious good humor. It is time to make his offering. He removes the package from inside his coat and hands it to the boy, who gingerly peels off the wrapping, not taking his eyes from Theodore until he has dropped the paper to the floor.

At first Theodore imagines that it is himself being unwrapped, the boy peeling away the lies of his life with cruel, deliberate slowness. But it turns out just as he had hoped: the boy's attention shifts completely, he forgets about Theodore, forgets all that he knows about the man, and gives himself over to childish delight. Already he is rolling the locomotive across the chipped ceramic tiles of the floor, bringing the wooden train to life with his voice: "Chuchu, chug-chug." He's a child again, thoroughly a child, with all his interest devoted to a toy.

In returning the boy to his childhood, Theodore has freed himself. The mother needs an explanation, and then Theodore will dance up the street and enjoy his easily won freedom.

"I wanted ..." Unexpectedly, he falters. But the woman nods, still unsmiling yet with a reassuring expression. She may not understand the reason for the gift, but she doesn't object.

Before he turns to leave Theodore squats, rests his elbows on his knees, and asks the boy his name. The child is too absorbed in play to notice, so Theodore asks again.

"The man wants to know your name." The woman blocks the train with her foot, and the boy stops just long enough to reply. "Tim," he snaps impatiently. Chuchu. Chug-chug.

Tim. It's a fine name, pristine and to the point. Tim. Theodore looks admiringly at the child bending over his new toy. The straw-haired boy called Tim. Theodore almost wishes the child belonged to him. His hand hovers an inch above the boy's head, palm open. Then he remembers where he is. He hastily bids good-bye with a slight nod, positions his hat, and leaves.

He descends the steps two at a time and hurries along the sidewalk with such high-stepping vigor that he looks like he might break into a skip. By the time he has reached number fifty-five, his pleasure has turned to glee. He's solved his problem, safely enclosed himself. Patting his coat collar to straighten it, he unlatches the picket gate and marches up the walk, thinking of young Tim, savoring the image of the boy bent over his wooden train. What is more satisfying than the sight of a delighted child? Theodore's only regret is that his own emotions are not equally instinctive, that he's had to forsake childish spontaneity along with his past. But he reminds himself that he's forty-nine years old, a fair representative of a type of man, precise, dependable, with distinguished tastes. He's completely filled himself in, and now, with the last threat averted, his mind is at ease. He has never felt more confident.

CONVICTA ET COMBUSTA

*T*he first thing I do in the morning every morning is recite the Lord's Prayer. I haven't made a mistake in seventeen years. Then I put on my gray linen skirt and lavender blouse with buttons and machine lace, the same clothes every day, rain or shine. In winter I feed Zerobabel my Indian myna bird and then open a book and wait for warm weather. In summer after I feed Zerobabel I leave my room and lock the door behind me. I don't always have a plan in mind. If I spend my time wandering inconspicuously, that's good enough. It's not as easy as you might think, even on Coney Island in the middle of summer. When you're nearly as old as Tammany Hall, people look twice. Especially children. They stop dead in their tracks and stare until their mothers slap their faces. For this they grow up despising women like me, as though we were to blame. But wait until they're old and just as poor, an eyesore, a symbol of all that's wrong with America. Maybe you'll be fortunate and never experience old age, but if you plan to take your time, you'd better start practicing the Lord's Prayer now, that's all I can say.

Because if you can't recite the Lord's Prayer from beginning to end without making a mistake, you will be condemned and burned alive at the stake. I'm inclined toward superstition, I admit it. All those books I've read. You know if you spend just two hours a day reading, in fifty years it adds up to an awful eight years and four months of precious time. I don't believe in witches. But I am scared nearly to death of being accused. You never can tell what a passionate believer will do, maybe kiss you on the lips, maybe shoot you in the head. Or maybe scream, *Witch!* I am scared nearly to death of being burned alive. Not that I believe in witches. But how can I tell what other people will believe?

Take my own father, for example, a cook at Tilyou's Surf House. One day he persuaded himself that he was a fish, and before the month was out he had drowned off Coney Island Point trying to prove it. And then there's the history to consider, Pope Innocent's bull of 1488 calling upon Europe to rescue the Church of Christ from witches and launching the slaughter that continues to this day: of women, it was said, who transformed themselves into cats and danced on the backs of black goats, women who roasted babies over a slow fire and with the fat that trickled down anointed the hair and beard of Satan, women who vomited needles, women who caused famines and plagues. And not only women. In Salem, Massachusetts, in 1692 nineteen witches were burned, including a five-year-old child and a dog. Pope Innocent, what do you think about that? A five-year-old child and a dog.

Four hundred and twenty-three years after the celebrated bull an old woman can't be too careful. You never know who is going to accuse you of bewitching his little girl, his wife, even the horse he's gunning for at Gravesend, double or nothing. You never know who is a witchfinder and who an ordinary cop on the beat. *Countrymen: Hang her! Beat her! Kill her!* Maybe they don't use these same words anymore, nor do they put you in a room, tie you to a chair, and wait for your familiar to appear in the form of a fly or a mosquito. Sometimes they don't say anything at all when they gather around you, they just poke you and snatch your purse. I know from experience. I don't carry a purse on me anymore, I don't carry anything at all except a dime for a malted milkshake from Nathan's, which I drink as I walk out to the end of the Iron Pier and back again. But here I am getting ahead of myself, I was telling you what I do in the morning, and I don't buy my milkshake until two in the afternoon.

What I do in the summer season after I leave Julius's,

where I have lived for seventeen years, is this: I walk along the sidewalk looking around like it's all a novelty to me and I am one visitor among thousands, no one special. There is so much to see: the El Dorado triple-decked carousel, Babar's Bathing Pavilion, the Stratton Hotel, the Elephant. If you have never seen the Elephant, with its four-foot-high glass eyes and legs sixty feet in circumference, you've missed one of Coney's feature attractions. There's a room in the trunk eleven feet high, eleven feet in diameter. "See you at the Elephant" is what men say, never women, you figure out why.

Then there's the Brighton Beach Hotel, where Mama worked after she was widowed, champagne on draft at twenty-five cents a glass. And up the street is the Manhattan Beach Hotel, the finest of them all because it is far away from the roughs and their doxies, the pickpockets, the confidence men, the till-tappers and moll-buzzers and rowdies. If I had the means, I would move to the Manhattan Beach Hotel. But means I lack, so I stay where I am, Julius's Boarding House, and spend warm-weather days walking through crowds, mingling, making myself as thin as air like the souls of stillborn children.

It used to be I'd go to Steeplechase when I grew tired of looking at the hotels. But it was at Steeplechase I had my purse snatched, one dollar twenty-nine cents. Lucky for me I kept the rest of my savings in a hole in the wall behind my bureau, otherwise I would have been reduced to beggary and the witch-hunters would have had an easy job. I was watching the metal horses slide toward the finish line, their riders whooping, the crowd whooping back, when I felt a tug and I looked down and saw the straps of my purse hanging from my arm like seaweed. A little boy squeezing through the crowd looked up at me, grinned as though we were in league together, and disappeared. I turned to watch the end of the race, then I walked home to Julius's.

What good would it have done to report what happened? I learned long ago from Mama to keep my mouth shut. But later that night I couldn't help thinking about that boy, and I wondered was he put up to the caper, was there some pineapple waiting for the loot, was he happy-go-lucky because he'd done a good day's work and wouldn't be beaten? He was dark-skinned, black-haired, maybe one of the Romany gypsies advertised on billboards in front of Luna. I thought so much about him that I stopped frequenting Steeplechase and went to Luna instead, at first to look for the gypsy boy and then to admire the elephant Topsy. I never saw that boy again, which was all right with me. What would I have said if I found him? What would he have done?

So for the next few summers I went to see the elephant. I'd say to Zerobabel, no one else, "I'm off to see the elephant." I've already explained: men are supposed to say this, not ladies. But Zerobabel is only a bird and it was our little joke. "I'm off to see the elephant," I'd say to him, and one day he said it back to me. "I'm off to see the elephant." He still says it, stupid bird, not out of spite, he doesn't mean any harm. He grows used to my company off-season and tries to impress me so I won't leave him alone in the hot weather. He doesn't know that I stopped going to see the elephant last year. I stopped going to Luna altogether, and here's why:

Topsy couldn't waltz or smoke a pipe or eat her meals from a table like Little Hip and some of the other elephants. She couldn't do much at all but trumpet mightily—for this she was a star attraction. An extravaganza wasn't complete until Topsy raised her trunk and blew. And whenever Topsy was in the arena, I stood behind the chain-link fence with everyone else who couldn't afford a bleacher seat.

I was there the first time Topsy went berserk, thinking to myself how safe I felt in such a captivated group of chumps, especially now that I no longer carried a purse. I was thinking I couldn't be more invisible than this, one crooked body in gray and lavender among hundreds. But an old woman should never feel safe, no one should feel safe as long as people can be persuaded to do evil. Who persuaded the man standing ringside with a shovel to throw a lit cigarette into Topsy's open mouth as she was trumpeting I don't know. But that's what he did, and Topsy stopped trumpeting and started screaming. The next thing I knew the man with the shovel was dangling like a wet shirt from one of Topsy's tusks.

But Topsy was the star of Luna's animal act, and who would sacrifice a legitimate operation because of an unpleasant accident? So after a suitable period of time had passed—two weeks—Topsy was trumpeting again. And I was back at the fence, standing in the push that had swelled because of Topsy's infamy. Man-killers are always great attractions.

Topsy wasn't going to let the summer pass, though, without tasting blood again. She waited for another provocation, and when one of the assistant trainers lashed a whip into her eye, Topsy killed a second man. Since this was during rehearsal, only the crew on hand were witnesses. Thompson and Dundy, Luna's owners, tried to keep the story out of the papers, and failing that, they decided to retire Topsy. It was the middle of August. Though Thompson and Dundy didn't say so, we all knew Topsy would be back in the arena next June.

We. Don't think I use the word casually. *We* was what I wanted to be—I was a child of Coney Island and for years had no life separate from the life of crowds. Then I grew old, and age deprives a lady of her place in the midst. But with Topsy at the center of attention and everyone a comer, I was once more *we* that summer, as anonymous as I'd been when I was young, a speck of color in the background. And the following winter, during those long, solitary hours in my room at Julius's, no one but Zerobabel for company, I tried to sleep and dream the crowd around me. "I'm off to see the elephant," Zerobabel would croak to help me along, and I'd be back at the chain-link fence, blending in beautifully.

And I was back again the next summer for Topsy's first performance, which never took place because Topsy decided to smash a foolish janitor who threw a peanut in her mouth. Smashed him flat as a flounder, so the rumor went, and as far as I'm concerned, there's nothing truer than a rumor, nothing more expressive.

So on the first Saturday of the summer season a notice was posted outside the arena announcing that the elephant Topsy had become irretrievably vicious and was to be publicly executed the Saturday next, at noon, admission ten cents. Now, being as I was an admirer of Topsy's, you might think I would have chosen to miss the final scene. But I did more than attend the public execution. I even paid the admission and sacrificed my malted milkshake. Don't think I ordinarily go in for such things. On the contrary. I attended the execution because I had a prophetic feeling—call it an intuition, it sounds less supernatural—that Topsy would survive.

I climbed to the top of the bleachers and found a seat. The woman in front of me wore feathers in her hat that blocked my view, white, frosty feathers, like the print of cold on my window in winter. I had to stand to see Topsy as she lumbered into the arena. Her trainer walked with his head bent, making it perfectly clear that he wanted no part of this but was a slave to his bosses, just as Topsy was a slave to him. The master showmen themselves, Thompson and Dundy, arrived wearing velvet top hats and tails, the dust smoking around their ankles as they strolled toward the center of the ring, poisoned carrots in their gloved fists.

At first I felt as though I'd lost my way, like one of the wild Coney rabbits you sometimes see hopping in circles along the beach. Unlike the rest of the audience, I had no appetite for public executions. But when Topsy stubbornly kept her mouth closed, refusing Thompson's carrots, and the crowd began to cheer, I felt fine, in harmony, you might say, with the general mood. We were on Topsy's side. We wanted the elephant to live. After three quarters of an hour had passed and Thompson and Dundy had failed to nudge, thrust, or stuff the carrots into Topsy's mouth, they announced that the show was over and that they would try again the following Saturday.

We filed out of the ring, only a few among us grumbling that they had spent ten cents to see an execution and since there hadn't been any execution they wanted their money back. The rest of us were thoroughly pleased and ready to spend another dime to witness the indomitable Topsy outwit those blockheads again. The sweetest music in the world was Topsy's trumpeting as her proud trainer led her back to her pen.

All through the week the elephant ring was closed while workmen built a huge scaffold. Word spread that Topsy was to be hanged. I could have told those men to save their breath. On Saturday I spent another dime and watched as Thompson and Dundy and various assistant trainers tried to pull and push the elephant up the steep plank to the platform. Topsy wouldn't budge without her trainer, though, and he, following the animal's example, refused to collaborate. Thompson finally announced that if they couldn't lead the killer elephant to death, they would bring death to the elephant. Thompson is an insane lush, everybody knows the truth, and I heard the madness in his voice. I knew he meant to carry out the execution—from that moment on Topsy was doomed.

Still I paid my dime the third week, don't ask me why, I knew there was no hope left. We gathered around Topsy's cage and watched silently as workers wrapped her legs in chains. In the right leg of the Elephant Hotel there is a tobacco shop, in the left leg there is a jungle diorama. Wrap chains around the Elephant Hotel and pull the switch, see what happens. What happened to Topsy that day when they pulled the switch and sent twenty-five thousand volts through her was smoke poured out of her ears and mouth, out of her joints, through the hide, her eyes melted like candy into syrup, and she stood as still as the Elephant Hotel itself for five, maybe ten seconds and then collapsed forward and flipped onto her side.

Five, maybe ten seconds. To the elephant it must have lasted ten thousand years.

I never went back to Luna. I wandered along the sidewalk and sat on benches and watched the seagulls and bathers. People noticed me, some of the guilty idlers began to leave handouts on the bench beside me—half a sandwich, a penny, a bottle of pop. Once they recognize you it's the beginning of the end. So I was grateful for nightfall when people didn't have the time or take the time to notice. You see, at heart I'm a society girl, I like people, if only I trusted them. And always after dark my eyes would wander to the three-hundred-and-seventy-five-foot-high tower rising from the middle of Dreamland.

Dreamland was Coney Island's third amusement park, the newest, boasting twice as many turnabouts as Luna's, twice as many tunnels-of-love and shoot-the-chutes, and a Lilliputian village with three hundred midget inhabitants. I had never been to Dreamland and never planned to go. It was lit by one million incandescent light bulbs. The white tower at its center glowed as though it were on fire, a burning stake. If such a thing as I have described could happen at Luna, what could happen at Dreamland?

What could happen? Who was it who wrote, "Curiosity is the master passion"? I couldn't spend the rest of my life wondering, I had to take a few chances, especially now that I had so little to lose. On the first day of the season I woke up with a premonition that this summer would be full of adventures. Since I knew what I'd find at Steeplechase and Luna, the only place left for adventures was Dreamland.

The dime tucked into the top of my stocking was the last of my mama's legacy. Whatever you might say about my mama, as a mother she was blameless. She always cooked my dinner or else brought me a hogie from the hotel kitchen, she warned off any roving lechers, and she bequeathed an inheritance that she thought would keep me to the end of my days. How could she have foreseen that I would live so long? In the weeks since I've spent that dime, I've made ends meet one way or another. If worst comes to worst, I'll sell Zerobabel—I'll take him over to the lobby of the Elephant and auction him off. In such a place the price I get for him will far exceed his value. I may not have much sense about money, but I know about men and their humors. All those years spent watching and listening. Maybe I should write a book.

But I was telling you about the first eventful day of the summer. With Dreamland as my destination, I locked Zerobabel in my room and went out to bide time. The park was nothing until night, its whitewashed lath and staff as comfortless as asphalt. Only after darkness had fallen and one million bulbs were lit did the park deserve its name.

My first milkshake of the summer tasted just like the last milkshake from the summer before, chalky, rich with malt. The sky looked like last summer's sky. The crowds looked like the same old crowds. This has always been reassuring: despite the innovations, you'll find the same kinds of people in the same giddy mood year after year. I wanted to be in the mood of the crowd like I'd been when Topsy had made fools of her executioners. But by mid-afternoon I'd spent my mama's last dime and I was feeling sour. Maybe even then, in the back of my mind, I was thinking about betraying Zerobabel.

Darkness came at last and improved my spirits. I stood up and strolled along with the rest of humanity, then turned toward the entrance of Dreamland, where a giant plaster Adam straddled the threshold. As soon as I was inside I understood why I'd stayed away from Dreamland. However magnificent its skyline was at night, inside it was Luna's inferior—it may have had more rides and booths, but it lacked the population. The boulevard beside the lagoon was too spacious, the crowds too sparse. The barkers couldn't collect a push for their shows, the pick-pockets couldn't hustle, the mitt-joints were empty, and the fortune-tellers sat on stools outside the tents, cooling themselves with fans made of playing cards.

If anyone had asked me for advice, I would have said to cut the scale by half. But the man behind Dreamland, the Senator he was called, had long since decided immensity would be the draw. If he wasn't going to listen to me, he might have taken a lesson from his own park. What do you think was the main attraction? Not Madame Morelli and her seven leopards. Not the Alpine train or the flotilla of gondolas. Dreamland's most popular show was the Incubator Babies, where the main players all weighed less than three pounds and slept in glass boxes. The hospitals didn't want the Incubator Babies, no more than a church wants freaks among its congregation. Which was why the Senator got them cheap.

Dreamland had been designed to be better, brighter, more excessive than Luna and Steeplechase, but it failed to draw the numbers that would have made the excess profitable. It had been open for three years when I first entered that day through Adam's portal. It would be quick in dying. I knew it was dying just as sure as I'd known Mama was dying way back when. She'd do her face every day and head off to work, but the eyebrows were crooked, the lipstick smeared. Toward the end I cooked her scrambled eggs, but feeding her was like trying to reach the gong on the high-striker. Each day I hit the teeterboard, each day the rubber ball fell further from the mark until I couldn't make it rise at all.

Despite one million incandescent bulbs, by 1911 Dreamland was on its last breath. From the outside it was still a spectacle, but up close it was pitiful. Like Mama. Like my daddy the fish. Like anyone near the end, I guess. And when you're an object of pity, you can be sure you're an object of contempt as well. So if you're not going to hide in some dark crawl space and go quietly, privately, like a blind old cat, expect to die a fiery death in the manner of Topsy.

Outside the building with the Incubator Babies, the Wild Man from Borneo announced the feeding schedule. Without a nickel for admission I had to be satisfied looking at the flash on the walls, the valentines and photographs of babies as small as the palm of a large man's hand. In the animal arena Captain Bonavita whipped his twenty-seven lions into order. I heard their roaring, like the sound of waves crashing against the pilings of the Iron Pier. In front of the gates of the Lilliputian Village a midget invited people to enter and threatened them with retribution when they walked by.

There was no sign that the Senator had plans of closing Dreamland's doors and giving up. Instead, he was still trying to revamp the enterprise, and that night a crew striped the white tower fire-engine red. But just as no shark will find a cure for old age any day soon, no senator will make a dying amusement park inviting. I could have told them what was going to happen, but I would have made myself an easy target—a prophet is always the first to be accused. So I minded my own business and thought about the lesson to be learned from Dreamland.

What I couldn't have told them was when and how, and here's where the story gets fantastic. You'll think I'm lying when I tell you I had nothing to do with the fire that broke out in Dreamland in the middle of that night. I don't blame you. I think I'm lying. My vision of what would happen nearly coincided with the event, maybe even caused it.

I left Dreamland shortly before midnight, thinking about the smoke that one day would pour through the Creation entrance and seep through the white walls. Shortly after midnight the fire began. This is my testimony. I no longer believe in my innocence because I no longer know what innocence is.

I'd seen West Brighton burn in 1899. I'd seen the Bowery go up in smoke in 1903. I'd even paid admission to the burning ruins of Steeplechase after the fire of 1907. So why I slept through this fire, the fire of fires, the fire that might very well have been my own perfidious work, I don't know. They say the fire began in Hell Gate, where a crew was caulking a water spillway. A light bulb popped in the heat, someone kicked over a tub of hot pitch, and in a few seconds Hell Gate was in flames. They say that the fire spread first to the building housing the Incubator Babies but that all the babies were saved. They say that over eighty animals perished but that the Shetland ponies were spared because their heroic keeper stayed with them and fought the flames single-handedly. The burning tower collapsed at three A.M., and the cascade of sparks poured like water from a faucet. I slept through most of the night and woke up only when I heard the distant popping sound of gunfire.

By the time I arrived at Dreamland, the fire had almost burned itself out and the only animal to escape from the arena—a Nubian lion called Black Prince—was already dead. He had been cornered at the top of the Rocky Road to Dublin Railway. They fired twenty-four bullets into his head, and when he still kept twitching, they split open his skull with an axe. I learned all this from bystanders gathered around the lion's carcass, which had been dragged out to the sidewalk in front of Adam.

While I stood there a man called for a pair of pliers— I recognized him as a local carny who worked the roller coaster over at Luna. A few minutes later pliers were produced. I watched the carny take the pliers first in his left hand, then in his right, and open them slowly as though testing their resistance. I heard what I thought were sirens. Only later did I realize that the sirens had long since stopped and that these were the last shrieks of the animals burning to death in the park. I watched the carny pry open Black Prince's bloody lips. He secured the pliers around a tooth and jerked it out by the root. I almost expected the lion to leap up. The carny pulled another tooth. If I hadn't known any better, I might have thought the Nubian's teeth were being extracted for sanitary purposes. But I am a child of Coney Island and understand this mean world of cons and pitches and shills—anything that comes free becomes a souvenir and sooner or later will cost a pretty penny. The carny didn't quit until all of the lion's teeth were in his pocket. And when the crowd dispersed, I did too.

What goes through a mind when the flames have wrapped around the body? That's what no one will ever figure. Still, I can't help but think about much of anything else these days. It doesn't look like the Senator is going to rebuild Dreamland or even open up the ruins to the public. Which everyone agrees is a shame. Though Dreamland was only a poor imitation, something essential has been lost.

I still go out for a daily perambulation and a milkshake, if I'm lucky enough to find a dime. Then I come home and sit in my gray skirt and lavender blouse waiting for the word to spread like Dreamland's conflagration. I'll be accused—rightly or wrongly, it doesn't make much difference because the end is the same. What goes through the mind? I keep wondering. Any mind. Maybe I will sell Zerobabel tomorrow and with the money purchase one of Black Prince's teeth. With the few hairs left on my head I'll make a necklace and I'll be wearing the tooth when they come for me.

They will come, I have little doubt, just as they came for the others. And when I hear the doorknob turn, I will start reciting the Lord's Prayer. Maybe I will wait until they are in the room to be sure they hear every word. I will recite the Lord's Prayer without making a mistake. And then, to spite them, I will say it backward.

You Must Relax!

What our grandmother keeps in her walk-in closet: silk in pastel pink and blue and peach, *crêpe de chine*, chiffon, *mousseline de soie*, tulle, satin ribbons, boleros, corsets, hats with feathers, hats with cloth flowers, cloches, beaded caps, tunics, hobble skirts, gray wool suits, evening dresses, and dressing gowns.

Lately, Granny Madge has taken to locking herself in her closet. She sits on a wooden folding chair for hours, counting aloud in a low, monotonous voice. While she counts we know that she is recalling those important moments that she would rather forget—it is her punishment to remember, she says. St. Paul de Vence, for instance, 1923; a garden party, a stone wall and morning glories wet with dew, slippery slate steps. She remembers exactly what she wore that day: her lemony silk dress and straw hat shaped like a chanterelle. Her husband wore gaberdine. Her little boy Lou, our papa, wore knickers and a peasant blouse. Lou, his fists the size of apricots. He insisted on carrying the trifle himself though his arms couldn't reach entirely around the wide glass bowl. Layers of wine-soaked sponge biscuits, ratafia cakes, whipped cream, fresh raspberries. He staggered beneath the weight. Still, such challenges are important to children, Madge believed, so she let him carry the bowl, guided him by the shoulders up the steps to the terrace, the brim of her hat covering Lou in shadow, his face pinched in a knot of concentration, reddening as he neared the trellis canopy. His mother didn't notice his gasps, though, because as she climbed the final steps she heard a familiar voice coming from the far corner of the terrace. She couldn't make out what it was saying but she recognized that voice. Five years had passed since she'd heard it last. If a century had passed, she still would have known it instantly.

In an attempt to avoid the meeting, she backed down a step, away from the terrace. She jostled Lou ever so lightly, reason enough for him to give up his impossible effort. He let his arms go limp as he mounted the top step, and the bowl—a punch bowl that was an heirloom two generations old, glass engraved with an intricate floral design on the island of Murillo—the bowl, the trifle, the candied violets, slipped from the little boy's arms and crashed onto the terrace.

The next awful minutes are like a news photo in our grandmother's mind, an artful composition posing as the truth. She remembers: the embarrassed glances directed at her from three sides, the top of her son's bowed head, the splattered trifle that looked like the eviscerated carcass of a large rabbit, white fur and bruised, purplish gut, the puddle of raspberry blood already coagulating. In her memory she stands apart, watches herself as though she were another guest, sees a woman mesmerized, sees a boy with eyes squeezed shut trying to will away the accident and make time go backward, sees, then, a middle-aged man come toward her.

He'd grown a beard, a black, patchy chin-beard; he'd put on weight, so his face had lost its slender, oval shape, and he wore a monocle as though he were a great scholar when in fact he was nothing but a showman, a pretender who flaunted knowledge, exploited knowledge, used knowledge as an alchemist uses chemistry. Perhaps the five years since she'd seen him last, since she'd renounced him in an attempt to claim her self-respect again, had matured her so thoroughly that she could judge with critical detachment the doctor who had once entranced her. Or was it that he had changed, had lost his honest manner, had replaced homeopathic promises with affectation? The doctor five years earlier had seemed a wise man, almost a prophet; in his place, Madge saw a hypocrite.

He walked across the terrace toward her, the one

animated figure in the frozen picture, moved as steadily as a flame burning down the stem of a matchstick. He squatted in front of the shattered bowl and began picking out fragments of glass as though this would somehow help, carefully removed one sliver after another, and collected the pieces in a pile at his side.

Finally Lou opened his eyes, saw that his wish hadn't come true, time hadn't reversed itself, he'd failed miserably, and even worse, no one reproached him. They were too full of pity to reproach him. And now a bearded man knelt before him, a grown man on his knees; nothing Lou had done had ever produced such dramatic consequences. He looked up at his mother, not quite believing that he was responsible, looked back at the man, looked at his mother, saw an unfamiliar expression (and our grandmother, in her memory, sees everything now through her son's confusion), looked at the faces of strangers, looked at the man's hands again, then closed his eyes because he couldn't bear it anymore and began to scream.

His screams demanded action. There were brooms to be fetched, dustpans to be filled, Madge's husband, who had dallied at the bottom of the steps with the host and only now appeared, needed an explanation, Madge needed reassurance ("No doubt it would have been delicious, Madame Whitcombe"), the boy needed a biscuit, the doctor needed a towel. For some reason the hostess handed the towel to Madge first, so she was obliged to pass it to the doctor, who deliberately grabbed her hand along with the cloth, held her even when she tried to pull away, held her for so long and gazed at her with such offensive intimacy that for a second time a hush fell across the terrace, the guests stared, our grandmother blushed. It was a more fatal accident than a ruined trifle, this inopportune joining of hands.

Lou had taken refuge underneath his mother's out-stretched arm, and the image of the three—the woman, the doctor, the boy in between—provided all the proof that anyone who ever had suspicions could have wanted. And they did have suspicions, Madge knew. Five years earlier people had whispered about her frequent consultations with the doctor, had wondered why her husband allowed her to go to Nice without an escort. But jealousy was as foreign to her husband as the French language had been to Madge during her first year abroad. She had been forced to learn French, though, since her husband's touring agency kept him away for weeks at a time. And now her husband would be forced to learn a new language: the language of jealousy. Not because the doctor looked at his wife with such ferocious interest; not because they continued to hold hands long after the interval proper for a greeting. While others saw proof, her husband would have a revelation: the woman, the doctor, the boy. As unarguable as simple addition. The boy, with his

coxcomb of black hair and his large, wide-set brown eyes,
his low forehead, his impish, pointed chin, was the obvious sum of two parts.

The doctor had damned Madge forever, had intended
as much, she believed. Surely he must have known that
she and her husband would be at this garden party. Four
years ago he'd moved his practice from Nice to London,
was now on his way to Lake Como for a holiday, had
obviously delayed the last leg of the trip so he could be
here, so he could see Madge, lovely Madge, "as beautiful
as ever," he murmured, and finally released her.

She wiped her palm, wet from perspiration, on the side
of her dress, gave him a nod, and pushed her son around
the broken bowl and away from the stranger who was his
natural father. Though everyone else knew the truth,
even her husband—yes, her husband knew best of all—
her son must never know.

And with nothing more to watch but much to discuss,
the guests regrouped into neat patterns of colors that
seemed to Madge both haphazard and carefully designed,
like tinted glass in a kaleidoscope. While they didn't talk
about her directly, through the next hour the men smiled
at her with oblique amusement and the women kept
glancing from husband to wife to doctor, their eyes drawn
by some irresistible force. The force of scandal. In private parlors and bedrooms gossip would flow from these
people, her gentle Catholic friends, gossip would take the

place of the trifle as their dessert, gossip would enrage, fatten, delight them, would give their insignificant lives meaning. Not only had the doctor calmed Madge's fraught American nerves five years earlier, not only had he given her back her peace of mind, he'd given her a bastard son as well. Not just a son. A son with Jewish blood. He'd given a Jewish baby to a Protestant adulteress—mixed blood, no good would come of the boy, he'd suffer for his mother's shame, and wasn't it more than coincidence that he'd dropped the precious glass bowl, a trial run for future catastrophes, the first of many acts of violence to follow? Who could blame the doctor? He was just a man, with a man's instincts, a man's vulnerabilities.

Other women in the village had traveled to Nice by themselves to consult the famous doctor; other women had let him touch them as no one but their husbands should have touched them. But only Madge had borne his child. She knew what they would say about her behind her back; she knew that these self-proclaimed libertarians made pets of Jews, even on occasion made love to them. They wouldn't condemn her for love. But there was the question of purity. She had brought an impure child into the world, and though they could forgive him, they could never forgive her. She didn't have to rely on malicious confidantes to know what her friends were thinking. They would satisfy their hunger, would obscure the actual object of their prejudice by directing their thrilling, rapacious hatred at her.

Was our grandmother making unfair assumptions about these people? No fingers had been pointed, after all; no accusations had been made. To some observers this gathering might have held no secrets—once the trifle had been cleared up, the guests resumed their separate conversations, mingled, told jokes, ate and drank and eventually dispersed. A garden party like any other garden party. This was one interpretation, and probably a few uninformed guests believed it. Maybe most of them believed it and hardly gave Madge a second thought. But the guest with the most at stake learned at this party that he'd been betrayed by his wife. Though he would never confront her directly, from that day on he would begin to withdraw behind a silent, brooding mask, would pretend that he no longer cared about her or Lou until he drove himself to despair with the lie.

They forced themselves to linger at the party. Madge's husband wandered around the rim of the terrace, admired the roses and foxglove and held out his empty glass whenever the waiter came by with an open bottle of champagne. Madge strolled from group to group, nodded politely when opinions were exchanged, brushed her fingers through her son's hair, caressed his cheek, ostentatiously displayed her love. Whatever her friends said about her, they couldn't deny that she loved her son.

After a suitable length of time the family departed, managing a discreet exit. Yet even as they descended the slate steps Madge sensed, and perhaps her husband sensed as well, that they would never appear together in public again.

*O*ur grandmother is sitting in the dark. She used to spend her days in the living room playing solitaire or staring out the window. Now she just sits in the dark closet and counts aloud, higher and higher.

Once in a while she stops counting and listens. Or she remembers listening, though it is almost the same thing. She remembers listening for the sounds of footsteps, cowbells, a dog's bark, anything that would destroy the illusion of solitude. She spent the summer of 1923 roving the hills with her son, gathering dandelion leaves and sorrel for salads that would never be made, nettles for stews, rosehips for syrups. After a rain she would forage in the pine groves for puffballs the size of turnips, full of brown, powdery spores. And boleti, satanic boleti with spongy red caps. She would set the deadly mushrooms on the windowsill out of her son's reach, and when they had withered, she would throw them out and pick more. That summer she enjoyed a rare freedom, though at the time such freedom seemed a trap. No matter how far she walked, she never reached a place satisfactorily remote, where she could have screamed as loud as she pleased, where she could have spit and danced naked. She was

afraid, perpetually afraid of being discovered, afraid most
of all of being discovered by the one who always accompanied her: her son.

Our father still speaks of these days as the finest of his
childhood. No lessons to study, no obligations, nothing
to do but leap over logs and bathe in shallow creeks,
throw pebbles at fish, pet the whiskered muzzles of
ponies, catch toads and grasshoppers. Ordinarily his
mother was a grave, didactic presence, an unrelenting
moral supervisor. *Energy, application, painstaking patience
and persistence.* These were the words Madge used to
repeat to her son. But that summer she acted as though
idleness were the sole objective. The sun burnt Lou until
he was "as crisp as a pygmy, and wasn't he just as illiterate
and wild!" Or so Aunt Sarah—Madge's sister—
declared when she arrived in St. Paul de Vence to take
charge. Someone had to take charge while the man of the
house was off charting next year's tour through Greece.
With the difficult arrangements to be made—hotels to
be booked, coaches to be hired—he was so busy that he
didn't even have time to write to his wife. In his absence,
the usually orderly household had deteriorated. Weeks
before Aunt Sarah arrived Madge had dismissed the
cook, and she didn't even notice that spiders had spread
their webs across the doorways. Her son's mop of hair
became so tangled that she would simply pat her hands
over the top without brushing it, bills remained sealed,

and one afternoon she lifted the cloth from the birdcage and discovered her neglected pair of canaries lying on the floor of the cage. In their nest she found a cluster of speckled eggs.

That same day she wrote a long letter to her husband and addressed it to the pension where he was staying in Athens. She put her son to bed early and prepared supper for herself—a piece of chevre, day-old bread, a fennel bulb, claret, and boleti in cream. She ate three poisonous mushroom caps, laid down her spoon, and waited.

Rather, she continued to wait. She had been waiting all summer, and the stomach cramps at first were an exhilarating commencement: something was about to happen. She retired to her bedroom, propped herself up on her pillows, and opened a book about gardening. But the drawings on the page made her nauseous, as though the sensation of taste were located in her eyes, the illustrations nothing but wormy, putrid pieces of food. Mushrooms in cream.

She hurried to the toilet, pulled her dress up and her bloomers down, shat a thin, bluish liquid, rolled over onto her knees, and vomited. So this was life revealed: filthy, stinking, nothing noble about it, only pain and shit and bile. She retched again. Life leaked out, spilled, dripped, abandoned her. Madge had broken the trust, so life renounced its loyalties, left her hollow, or nearly so, and stuporous, drenched in sweat.

She managed to crawl back to her bed and almost immediately fell into a heavy slumber, only to wake an hour later for the second exodus: pain and shit and bile. But still enough life remained to keep the vital organs working, and though she returned to bed the second time convinced that she was dying, she woke at noon the following day to find that she hadn't died. And it was a good thing, wasn't it? With the cook gone someone had to prepare meals for her son. Her poor boy. Better for a boy to have an imperfect mama than no mama at all, she told herself as she ran her finger along the curved ridge of his spine. Her sweet child must have crawled into bed with her early in the morning, had forced himself to lie absolutely still so he wouldn't wake her, and had fallen asleep.

Her joints throbbed, her brain seemed squeezed in a vise, but she managed to push herself to her feet. Downstairs in the kitchen she patched together a meal for her son of sliced peaches and cheese. Not until she had set his plate on the table did she notice the leftovers. A skin had formed on the cream; an inky brown leaked from the remaining mushrooms, and the color had spread like cracks in ice. Her son could have climbed up on the chair and helped himself. She might have poisoned her own son, her only child, might have even, in her despair, left the pan of mushrooms out for him—a madwoman's attempt to destroy the witness. She was insane, clearly, and if anyone had been checking on her these last weeks, they would have surely committed her to an asylum, locked her out of reach of the boy, restrained her so she could do no harm to anyone.

She let the eggs grow rubbery and cold and her son sleep while she wrote to her sister, who was married to an antique dealer and lived in Sussex, inviting her to visit. Then she poured the mushrooms into a square of cheese-cloth folded to triple thickness, dropped the bundle into a burlap sack, and because she couldn't think how else to get rid of it, she buried the sack in the vegetable garden.

Madge didn't stay in Provence long enough to find out whether new mushrooms ever sprouted; a week after Aunt Sarah arrived, Madge's letter to her husband was returned unopened, along with a note from the owner of the Athens pension informing her that her husband had never arrived, had never even landed in Piraeus. It appeared that in Naples Madge's husband had boarded a ship bound for Greece but had disappeared en route. Whether he had fallen or had been pushed, no one knew. The captain had filed a report with the police in Piraeus, and he would keep the gentleman's trunk until further notice.

Madge traveled with her son to Piraeus to claim her husband's belongings; from Greece they took a steamer back to New York. She wore black tulle over her head and had her meals delivered to her cabin. She hardly touched the food. By then, a month and a half since she'd last seen her husband, she knew that though she was a widow her family of two would soon be joined by a third: before he had set out for Greece, her husband had made certain that he left something of himself behind.

She gave birth to a second son the following winter. She soon tired of the city and by spring she had made up her mind to move upstate. She chose Spragton as her home simply by closing her eyes and placing her finger on a map.

Our grandmother is sitting in the closet in the dark. She inhales deeply, holds the darkness in her lungs as a child might hold water in his mouth. To us, the closet smells like an elderly woman—a particular combination of perfumes and old fabrics, the smell as unique as a thumbprint, slightly stale but not unpleasant. To Madge, however, the closet smells of money. Whatever she wears, her wealth is obvious; she can't help it and would prefer to disguise the truth, though that would mean additional purchases, more money spent on new clothes that weren't so conspicuously dear, more money converted into less distinguished goods. Not that she was ever a spendthrift. Just the opposite. From the start she thought of every dollar spent as an investment—she spared no expense in the early years and she's been rewarded by high returns.

Still, she wishes that her affluence weren't so apparent. In the lightless closet she tries to differentiate between the smell of wealth and her own scent, but the air is saturated with purchases, articles that have only increased in value over time and that someday will be dispersed among the rest of us. Yes, she invested wisely—she knows that to her heirs, everything stems from this.

She exhales, inhales through her mouth with short, choppy gulps. She wonders whether she could choose not to breathe, could willfully close out the offensive smell, could hold her breath and still keep counting. It is comforting, but not comforting enough, to follow a sequence.

We are all proud of our grandmother. It wasn't with money—not entirely—that she gained influence. And her looks didn't "melt any hearts," as one ancient and slightly drunken Spragton dignitary had recently said to her in a fit of nostalgia. Her slight, girlish figure and tightly wound chignon would have served another woman better, a woman who was less severe than our grandmother, less demanding. No, Margaret Whitcombe conquered Spragton by doing what she does so well—by counting aloud one wintry afternoon five decades ago.

Between 1900 and 1930 the population of Spragton increased by 70 percent. Our grandmother was lucky to arrive when the inhabitants still welcomed strangers, and if our family would never enjoy the status of those descended from the original settlers, Madge did manage to become one of the town's most influential leaders. A widow, mother of two small children, a woman of independent means, not nearly as demure as she should have been, even tyrannical at times, without important connections and, evidently, with no intention of remarrying—who would have predicted in those early months that she would rise to such heights?

Of course, she didn't have to start from scratch. On top of her inheritance she had money from her husband's life insurance policy. She had an original Paul Poiret dress. And she had two disarming sons, Lou a would-be lady's man even at the age of five, our Uncle Harry a sanguine infant who rarely fussed, a mother's dream. Whatever doubts the people of Spragton had about our grandmother, her devotion to her sons was undeniable. With a family to support, Madge's aggressive manner could be excused, could even be admired. Still, she needn't have been so suspicious, really. Spragton was made up of plain, trustworthy people, neighbors who prided themselves on their honesty. Fair and square, no one surreptitiously jacked the price or tried to undersell a competitor, no one disguised terms with legal jargon, no one inflated the worth of services. Naive ethics, perhaps, but intentionally naive—greed was considered not an intrinsic human trait but an aberration: both the cheat and the customer who believed himself cheated were unnatural, especially the latter, since in this economy based on trust no one had to worry. Or so the typical Spragton businessman believed. No one dared to cheat, no one dared to complain. Each small business was like a windmill, an intelligible source of power driven by an unpredictable, external element. Blades turned with an easy whir and hum or did not turn at all, depending on the weather. The essential thing was to invest your money well.

At first the board members of the major bank in town treated our grandmother warily. She had enough money to cause trouble, enough to know the pleasures of wealth, enough to want more. They would, they assumed, have to reckon with her. But once they had decided that her apparent ambition was nothing but pronounced maternal instinct, their doubts gave way to affectionate concern, though not yet to respect. Margaret Whitcombe had to win their respect.

"Affectionately yours." With this, Velma Bartholomew, wife of Murrian, Chairman of the Board, signed the invitation. And she meant it, too, for Velma was a woman brimming with affection, a woman so adroitly officious that she gave the impression of belonging to whomever she was addressing, even in conversation poised her body in such a way—her back slightly arched, chin raised, eyes lowered—that she seemed on the verge of falling into the arms of whomever stood opposite.

At the Bartholomews' home one afternoon over fifty years ago, our grandmother stood opposite Velma, endured the gushing praise of this person she hardly knew, wearing all the while the distracted look of a mother who, with much reluctance, has left her young children in a stranger's care.

It was a small party, given in honor of those newcomers who hadn't arrived in Spragton looking for handouts. Among them, Madge was particularly deserving, by common vote the bravest pilgrim of them all—everyone wanted to do something for her, though in the three months since she'd been in town, she had made it clear that she would accept nothing for free. Unfortunate, the men agreed, that the widow was so testy.

Since she refused to hire an accountant to manage her finances, Murrian Bartholomew had to deal with her himself, though he relied on his wife to soften her hard edges, and he kept their meetings brief. Along with the others he felt great sympathy for the young widow. But when it came to business, she had shown herself to be unyielding and unrelenting, nimble, potentially vicious, "a witch, to tell the truth," he had confessed to the bank's vice-president once while Madge sat outside his office. And she had overheard—not every word but enough to understand from then on the precise nature of Spragton's affection.

Poor widow, devoted mother, witch. Give her a glass

of punch and let the wives take charge, let her prove that she can hold her own where she belongs, a lady among ladies. So Murrian privately reasoned that day at his party, and he led the men into his library. Here, away from their wives, the old guard could begin campaigning, which was the purpose of all of Murrian Bartholomew's parties. His fellow board members plied new, would-be investors first with bourbon, then with promises, assuring their interested listeners that whatever else was said about this northern outpost, the businessmen of Spragton never ran afoul. Fair and square. If Spragton had a motto, this would have been it: fair and square.

Though from the adjacent room Madge couldn't make out the particular negotiations taking place in the library, she had a talent for intuiting essences. She would have preferred to hear Murrian's sales pitch directly rather than through Velma. But resentment is useless for a woman, our grandmother believed. She thought it better to conform than to protest, better to take what she could given the restrictions, better to maintain her dignity. With energy, application, painstaking patience and persistence, a woman could do well for herself. Quite well. A woman could pose a formidable challenge.

Velma was admiring Madge's very handsome if somewhat passé beaded cap, when she interrupted to introduce her mother-in-law, "Lady Bart," a small, stooped old woman who obviously had meant to sneak past but now had to submit to her daughter-in-law's smothering embrace.

"Isn't she sweet," Velma said, smiling with such affection that her lips curled back to reveal gums the color of peat. "She'd fit on a spoon. Wouldn't you like to eat her for dessert!"

Lady Bart, the infamously fretful Lady Bart, four feet three inches high, seventy-nine years old, was, Madge would soon understand, the key to her own reputation. It took her only a few minutes to see the possibilities contained in this irascible miniature, who looked even smaller than she was because of her bent posture but whose eyes were huge and seemed to grow larger as she raised her head, the brown irises like liquid spilled on white cloth.

"Catholic, Missus?" Lady Bart wasted no time, and though Velma encouraged her with a nervous giggle to ignore the question, Madge was quick to reply.

"No, as a matter of fact."

She had the distinct sensation that the old woman was trying to appear as monstrous as possible. But Madge felt instead a similar fascination to what she had once felt watching the rolling eyes of an unbroken colt that was locked securely in its box stall, felt, too, that she was facing a distorted reflection of herself, perhaps a reflection of what she would become. She didn't recoil, and the old woman, realizing that this stranger was more resistant than most, softened.

"That's all right," she said with a shrug. "All roads lead to God."

From then until Lady Bart's death the following month the old woman and the young widow were committed friends; and by the end of the night Murrian Bartholomew no longer considered our grandmother a witch. On the contrary, he believed her to be the cleverest woman he'd ever met, a woman who managed to succeed where dozens of doctors, preachers, herbalists, and apothecaries had failed. Our grandmother, against all odds, gave sleep back to Lady Bart.

"She hasn't been well," Velma explained intrusively, stroked the old woman's gray tendrils of hair, smiled at her with affection.

But Lady Bart's story was her own to tell, and she pushed away Velma's hands impatiently. "They think I'm . . ." she said, tapping her temple with her forefinger. "Haven't slept for six months. Six months!" Clearly the old woman considered insomnia her unique talent. What had begun as a sickness had become a triumph—it wasn't that she had lost the ability to sleep, but she had conquered the need, and she never felt as alive, she insisted, as she did in the lost hours of the night. While the rest of the world slept, Lady Bart kept watch. If she didn't keep watch, who would know how much time had actually passed, or that time had passed at all?

"Can't trust clocks," she warned, taking Madge by the elbow, leading her away while Velma stared after the pair with astonishment and not a little anger. But Madge didn't notice Velma's anger. Tiny Lady Bart demanded her full attention. With a voice that sounded like toast being crumbled and fingers clenched so tightly around her arm that the next day she had bruises above her elbow, the old woman didn't give Madge a chance to hesitate.

In the front hall they took seats at one end of the long deacon's bench, Lady Bart chattering all the while about her remarkable ability. Six months. She hadn't slept for six months, and if Madge didn't believe her, there were others who would testify that since July Lady Bart hadn't even dozed. She might have reclined now and then, she might have shut her eyes and folded her hands across her chest, but her senses remained awake. Always alert, always listening.

She had heard the clock in the hall toll every hour of every day for the past six months, she had sat through every dusk, midnight, and dawn, had listened to rain, to sleet, to branches scratching the windowpane, had finally, after eight decades of ignorance, learned to live and would continue to live, defying sleep, defying death, emancipated, as she put it, from the tyranny of the body. She had rooted out the fear of death and so would not die from fear, which was why most people died—from the unspeakable terror of departure, an exhausting terror that shortens life, Lady Bart explained, her lips pursed, stretching the wrinkled skin of her face. Whatever we believe, whatever we think, whatever we attempt, we die—so why live in fear? Fear is blasphemous; through fear, the coward argues with God. Why bother arguing? Purge yourself of fear and you'll live twice as long or longer, you'll live as long as God wants you to live. St. Narcissus died at the age of one hundred and sixty-five, St. Anthony at one hundred and five, the Hermit Paul at one hundred and thirteen, and St. Simon, the Virgin's nephew, at the age of one hundred and seven, and only then because he was martyred. Most people kill themselves gradually, a whiskey in one hand, the supposedly rejuvenating serum of a heifer in the other, both poisons, both shocks to the system.

Lady Bart believed that sleep was a shock to the system, the devil's work. The problem, our grandmother reasoned, lay at the center of her logic. The old woman believed it her duty to prolong life but worried that if she relaxed for a moment life would be taken from her. Fear, this same blasphemous fear, was the inspiring force behind Lady Bart's insomnia. Afraid to lose control, afraid to sleep, she had disguised her fear as courage and considered herself more noble than others because of her efforts.

Even as Lady Bart prattled on, Madge devised a plan. She listened politely to the old woman's sermon on the near immortality of the terrestrial envelope and then proposed the wager that would mark the beginning of the end for Lady Bart: our grandmother boasted that she could cure any insomniac. If Lady Bart agreed to follow her instructions, she would, before the hour was up, be fast asleep.

Madge had never tried the mesmeric cure on anyone, nor had she given it much thought in the years since the doctor of Nice had massaged her own neck with his relentlessly seductive fingers. But "progressive relaxation" was as dependable as a tested recipe. If she failed she would leave Spragton and never return, she said—a vow made impulsively and dishonestly. If our grandmother had failed, she would have readily gone back on her word and stayed put. It was useless to try to escape, she knew by then. No matter what, she intended to dig in her heels and make Spragton her home. She would never run away again.

"You think you can do it?" The old woman gave a short laugh, more like the cough of a small, sickly dog. "You think you can put out the light in here?" She tapped her forehead. "Try! Go ahead, try!" What wicked pleasure Lady Bart took in the dare; how proud she was, this thin, inexhaustible woman who wanted to live forever. But if, as she claimed, she had conquered the need for sleep, the idea still tempted her. Madge tempted, and that afternoon Lady Bart began the slow withdrawal that for six months she had successfully forestalled.

Crafty Ulysses stopped the flow of blood with special incantations; the French physician Corvisart treated the Empress Josephine with pills of bread crumbs. Somewhere between these extremes of magic and delusion lies the science, or art, of hypnosis. The doctor—our grandfather—had been developing his own peculiar method when Madge was referred to him. Instead of treating his patients with drugs or sending them to costly spas, he believed "progressive relaxation" to be the most effective cure for nervous collapse. "You Must Relax!" became his byword and eventually the title of his book that received international attention. But Madge went to him in the early days of his practice, when he still called his treatments experiments. Madge was one of his most successful experiments. He groped (literally, in the final sessions, with the lights off, her blouse unbuttoned) and evolved a method "to quiet the nerve-muscle system, including what is commonly called 'the mind.' "

Obedient, cynical, but vaguely hopeful, Lady Bart followed Madge's instructions, lifted her feet onto the bench, and leaned back until her head rested against our grandmother's thigh. The aim, Madge explained, was "to cease contracting each and every muscle"—the doctor's exact words, and as she repeated them, she heard his voice, a disembodied voice, ingeniously persuasive. As she massaged the old woman's scalp, she repeated what she heard.

"Trust me. Keep your legs uncrossed and close your eyes gradually, bend your left arm at the elbow, let your hand fall limply from the wrist, now bend your hands backward, now forward, press your wrists against the bench, bend your neck, wrinkle your forehead, frown. Trust me. You are beginning to learn clearly what you must not do. You must relax, but first you must feel the tension, cultivate the muscle sense, understand what the slightest movement entails in order to lie still. Now try to lie still, do as I say, trust me. You don't trust me. If you trusted me you wouldn't blink, keep your eyes closed and breathe when I tell you to breathe, breathe in time with the numbers and keep your eyes shut tightly. Two, three, four—you'd sleep if you trusted me, you don't trust me yet, don't speak, considerable energy is wasted in unnecessary speech. Let it go, my dear, let it go. Five, six, seven. See how very simple it is. If you trusted me . . . do you trust me yet? Do you feel the slow spreading outward from the center? The body yearns to expand and finally to dissolve. Let it go. Trust me."

How long it took, Madge couldn't say—maybe thirty minutes, maybe two hours. But the old woman had fallen asleep long before Madge reached one thousand. She stopped counting, searched the oily, lined face for any stirring, but the lips were pressed together, the jaw set willfully, as though sleep were her decision and our grandmother merely an onlooker. But even with this illusion of self-determination Lady Bart would from now on be dependent upon Madge as Madge had once been dependent upon the doctor, deceived by him into believing that she could not fall asleep without him, could not, therefore, exist without him.

What a fool she'd been, but never, never again. She was in control this time, the purveyor of mesmeric freedom. She waited contentedly for someone from the party to venture into the hall and find the two women, the sleepless old matriarch at last asleep, her head resting on Madge's lap.

"It's nothing short of a miracle!" This was what they said, and our grandmother became a legend in Spragton, earning on a single afternoon respect that would last through her lifetime. But as if she had been granted one wish, only one, and had spent it on Lady Bart, our grandmother couldn't repeat the cure on anyone else. She tried, for years she tried.

Lately, she's been trying it on her own stubborn self, counting in bed, counting in the bath, counting in her closet with the door shut, the light off. We hear it day and night: the deep breaths and then the monotonous counting, the tedious ascents from one. We know better than to interrupt.

A BORDERLINE CASE

The Analytic Situation

*T*his is the story of K and B, analyst and patient; specifi-
cally, this is the story of their first session together,
before K had cured his patient, "dispersed" B, as he'd
say, helping him to become "more B than ever before." K
loved B, and if K hadn't had such a highly developed *le-
moi-peau*, he might have become irrevocably attached to
B "by cock, in mouth and arse" (B's description of his
own furtive activities). But K attached himself to his pen
instead, and for almost thirty years, on and off, through
three periods of analysis, he recorded B's anxious, obses-
sional narratives. Instead of admitting that he loved him,
he used B, turned his life into a notable if not ground-
breaking case history. K took credit for B's achievements

and ultimately for his happiness. B died a contented man, thanks to K, or so K would have it. And K died without ever once making love to B, neither buggering nor buggered by—a professional to the marrow. A prince. A lay analyst who believed himself a genius.

They met in 1953, when B was far less than he could have been, less B than B. He had a high-ranking post at the American Embassy in London at the time and had become increasingly adept at seducing young boys. Not boys who wanted him for himself but boys who wanted B's quid, boys on their way to a better life. "Escapades," as K referred to B's encounters with admitted distaste, discouraging B from supplying any graphic details, K stifling his own "clinical curiosity" because he feared that curiosity would make him B's accomplice, "an agent to his sexual prowling and practices." Though B was a "very narcissistic borderline psychopath," he was also a survivor, and if nibbling the foreskins of nameless youths gave him a sense of purpose, K wouldn't interfere. Just as long as B didn't talk about it. K didn't want to know. "There will be time enough to hear all that," he told B at their first meeting, and for almost thirty years he diverted B whenever he began to talk about "all that," until there was no time left—B died of heart failure in 1981, and K realized too late that his favorite patient had remained a mystery to him, on paper a sharply defined borderline case but in K's memory only the shadow of a man.

1953. K is twenty-four years old, at the start of a promising career; B is thirty-nine. K allows himself a quarter of an hour between patients so he can review his notes, pour a glass of fine Scotch whiskey, fill and light his pipe. The houseboy is responsible for meeting each patient at the front door and taking him up in the lift; the secretary escorts the patient into K's office as soon as the sideboard clock has chimed the hour. Ordinarily, a patient finds K waiting by the window, his back to the door. Not until the secretary has left does he turn to face his visitor, revolving slowly, his leather riding boots creaking, soles scratching against the wood, the sounds magnified by the vaulted ceiling. But on the day B arrives for his first consultation K is still in his chair, the letter from the referring analyst lying open on his desk.

"A homosexual who complains of a theoretical dislike of homosexuality. Prognosis: poor." So why bother? K wonders wearily, his mind so bored by the conjecture that he doesn't hear the knock. Why bother about anything? Why work, why talk, why write, why eat? In moments like these K indulges himself with the patronizing boredom that only the rich can afford, a boredom that, when flaunted, gives a man immeasurable control over those who bore him. K, a Punjabi Muslim, has more than enough wealth to keep himself entertained, but he values boredom, understands intuitively that boredom is as necessary as hunger, and he relishes the power gained with a well-timed yawn. He doesn't need to work and didn't choose this profession in order "to secure himself a place in the human community," every man's ambition, according to Freud. He works out of indifference—rather, works in order to channel his indifference, presides over his patients as he once presided at his father's side over Punjabi peasants.

On this sultry August day in 1953, however, K is caught off-guard. From the beginning B's case annoys him: a homophobic homosexual with doubtful therapeutic potential. K hasn't even had time to pour himself a drink. He looks up as the secretary knocks again, and a drop of perspiration slides into his eye.

B's first sight of the famous prince is of a thin young man behind a sprawling mahogany desk rubbing his fist against his eye. And from his side of the room K sees a blur, a watery ghost—uncharacteristically, he wants to see more. He rises abruptly from his chair and bumps his knees against the desk drawer, recognizes then, as the sharp pain travels along the nerve up his thigh, that this man B is extremely dangerous. B, despite the verdict from the referring analyst, already has the upper hand.

Not often in K's experience will a patient prove as witty as B, as daring, as "in the world," as B will say of himself, subtly proud of the intensity of his emotions, though long ago he developed a sardonic public manner, effective self-protection for a pederast who has worked both as a diplomat and as a coal miner. K, in contrast, swings back and forth between indifference and satisfaction, each day of his week organized carefully so that he can look forward to his pleasures without concern. B has never been able to plan ahead, much less to arrange his life so that he knows what to expect. His days are full of mishaps and coincidences, with few vacant moments for reflection. In a later session with K, B will compare himself to a small child abandoned in Piccadilly Circus, a child bumped and jostled, shoved, petted, squeezed, pinched, and pushed aside, a little boy without any sense of direction but determined to hold his own. B has taught himself to hold his own. K hasn't had the experiences that would make him B's equal. But K does have one advantage over B, an unqualified advantage: B may live more intensely than K, but K is more beautiful than B.

A polished diamond looks its value—the purer the stone, the more intricately it absorbs and refracts light, its crystalline surface suggesting to the human mind a fourth dimension, even the illusion of magic, as though, if we could see into the diamond, we would see the future. Young Prince K has a similar beauty: like a diamond, he looks his value; like a mounted, expertly cut diamond, he is inevitably the focus of any social gathering, startling enough to take your breath away. Even if you don't love K, you will love to gaze at him. By 1953 K has reaped much from his beauty, ascended quickly into the top ranks of his profession, to some a mere dilettante with a parasitical intelligence but in everyone's opinion a feast for the eyes. Perhaps his wealth has made prominence easier, but his beauty has made prominence possible. No photograph can evoke the immediate lure of the man in person. K's unique beauty rests mostly in the complicated dance of light upon his skin. When they know each other better, B will describe K's skin as "a lake of eucalyptus honey."

On their first meeting, as K moves from behind his desk, the heels of his riding boots clicking, his britches rubbing softly between his thighs, B gives in to the same passion that spectators lavish on movie stars. B falls in love with K at first sight, though he knows even then that he'll never possess him. K's beauty cannot be captured either by a stranger or by a lover—he is an illusion, a projection on a screen, all surface, a voluptuous imitation.

Still, even as he extends his hand, B imagines drawing his tongue along the curve where K's neck joins the shoulder, sliding down the side of his smooth skin, feeling the heat of his testicles, inhaling the residual smells of urine, semen, sweat, soap.

K the healer. Eucalyptus K. He can read B. He knows what the man is thinking, the laconic pansy, a puff out for a joy ride. Dangerous? Not as dangerous as K himself. K will make B panic, will throw him off-balance, will unnerve him, since B has already tried to do the same to K. K has a theory about people like B: "Instead of transference-readiness they tend to provoke or seduce the analyst into a tantalizing relation to their material," K will write, and though years later he will regret not involving himself "transference-wise" or "interpersonally" with B, from the beginning of the treatment he is determined to defend himself against seduction, not because of professional etiquette but because he considers himself too valuable for the likes of B, too valuable for anyone—with the exception of his fiancée, a prima ballerina—in ugly London town.

The men shake hands firmly, efficiently, and K motions toward a small oak table. He talks with new patients here before he moves them to the couch, first intimidates them with a face-to-face interrogation before he lets them spin on their own. But B proves too nimble for K—he walks past the table, sits at the end of the couch, crosses his legs at the ankles, and says, "Of course you want to know about my childhood."

Without a word K takes a seat in the rattan chair by the raised end of the couch, the least comfortable chair in the room, his "working-chair," as he calls it, preferring it precisely because it is so uncomfortable. A responsible analyst must stay awake and alert, an effort not as easy as it might seem, since the ambiance of the analytic situation is so conducive to sleep: voices droning on and on, words blending like musical notes until the analyst hears only the enervating melody, his eyes close, his head starts to nod, he sags and eventually topples from his chair. Such a fall would make K the laughingstock of the British Psychoanalytic Society, despite his good looks. Note-taking helps K to fend off sleep, and the chair keeps him from relaxing. No patient has ever found cause to fault him for inattention; he always appears assiduous if not entirely captivated, always looks as though he has an opinion about the matter at hand. Suave K, sophisticated K, will never be the object of laughter. He carries himself with an elegance that equals his fiancée's. Like his future wife, a dancer with the Royal Ballet, K is virtually incapable of awkwardness.

B, obviously to K, would prefer to spend his time lying on beds, on chaise longues and analysts' couches, torpid and engorged, like a boa that has just swallowed a small rat. He is an American. K despises Americans, a classless, cultureless people, their civilization representing the nadir of history. Yet he finds himself drawn to them, fascinated by these reptiles that don't chew their food. Perhaps it is a coincidence that in a later session B will recount a dream in which he shed his skin "just like a snake." Or perhaps K himself in some forgotten aside will make the comparison first.

With a manicured thumbnail K pushes the cap off his pen and records B's leading statement. Of course K wants to hear about B's childhood. Of course. "Affectless," K scribbles in the margin of the notepad as B lifts his feet onto the couch and reclines. K writes furiously, trying to keep up with B, while B describes three important experiences from his childhood. B is K's last patient of the day, so K doesn't bother to draw the therapeutic session to its normal close. Except for one terse comment to steer B away from the subject of perversity ("There will be time enough . . ."), he lets this arrogant Yankee talk until the supply of analytically pertinent (from B's perspective) and charmingly outrageous childhood memories has been depleted.

Finally, B licks his lips, parched from over an hour's worth of monologue, and falls silent. K exploits the silence, extends it, keeps B waiting for a response. A breeze ripples the edge of the window drape, the silky maroon color appearing almost fluorescent in the light. The flat spans the entire fifth floor, and by late afternoon the front room smells of exhaust from idling traffic on the busy street below. But this main room of the flat, the treatment room, faces the back, and the rich scent of the summer's second bloom of roses is in the air today: Amber Queen roses, Pacemaker and Harriny roses—K can name them all because he himself ordered them. K leaves nothing to chance, designs his world as if it were a stage set. Muslim piety, whiskey, and horses: these are the main elements, and everything else is filigree.

He breathes softly, and B begins to shift on the couch, bending his legs, holding up one arm and letting the wrist go slack, clenching his fingers, opening them, grinding his palms together. Then all at once he looks up with an expression less smug than before, eyes narrowed, corners of his lips turned down in a kind of pout, as though he is about to beg K to do something, to say something, above all to cure him. For the last hour and a half B has been trying to seduce K with his unconvincing attempt at free association, secretly inviting the young prince to test his patient's virility; K, however, will make it perfectly clear that B shall never earn a place on his list of pleasures. He keeps B waiting, pretends to be deep in thought while privately he gloats, enjoying his privileges as jury and judge. Only when B exhales loudly and swings his feet to the floor does K finally say: "What else have you rehearsed for me?"

It should end here. But right then B looks with such pathetic surprise, the look of a man who has been hurt time and time again but still doesn't believe in cruelty, that K can't help it: he reaches out and touches his patient on the shoulder to console him. Immediately he regrets it. With his hand resting on B, the muscles taut beneath his fingers, K is as helpless as B was a moment ago, unable to pull away, unable to convince himself that such contact has no lasting significance. *What else have you rehearsed?* The impact of his ill-timed comment has been lost; he is stuck to B's surface, on the verge of complete annihilation. In the few seconds before he is swallowed whole, K begins to discover the true meaning of panic for himself.

B Takes In His Surroundings

Among the many images in K's office B notices: a four-by-six-inch etching of the Bridge of Sighs, a Cubist painting of a cityscape, a Giacometti-style female figurine on a side table, a diploma from the University of Lahore, a certificate from the British Psychoanalytic Society, a shelf with six ribbed tumblers and a decanter, a coke fireplace, a white polo cap on the hook attached to the door, a marble polo-ball paperweight on the desk, a felt blotter, an ornamental ink stand and fountain pen, three photographs—one of K as a teenager standing between a white man (his tutor, B assumes) and his horse, one of K with his father, one of K alone in front of what B recognizes as the main bazaar in Lahore (B has been to Lahore twice on diplomatic missions)—a stack of empty file folders, a desk chair on wheels, a small Persian rug, a sea chest, four oak dining chairs upholstered in red leather, an oak sideboard, a telephone, a bronze nude Galatea with arms outstretched and a clock face in her belly, a small table beside the couch, a box of tissues on the table.

In Which B Boldly
Imagines a Conversation Between
K and His Tutor

"Are there not Western nations, I might ask—excuse me for a moment, sir, I must give my Anarkali a sugar cube. Every afternoon I bring her a sugar cube. One day I forgot, you know, and I hadn't been astride her for two minutes before she threw me. Would you like to ride her? She's particular, my Anarkali, you have to win her approval. Here, you feed her the sugar. You're not a horseman, I can tell. Hold your hand flat, like this. You see, I'm supposed to learn from you, but maybe you shall learn something from me, too. They say I'm precocious. Do you want to hear the truth, sir? My father prefers me to my brothers and sisters. This is why I'll be your only pupil. And this is why Anarkali belongs to me now. She used to belong to our neighbor, an Englishman like you, but much richer—he owns the fields that you saw to the left of the road as we came from the station. We own the fields to the right. I wanted to ride Anarkali, but Mr. Brooks wouldn't let me near her—he thought her too high-strung and was worried that I would be injured. So my father bought her from him. Perhaps it disturbs you that my father has more than one wife? Perhaps you would prefer to travel in a taxi instead of in our tongo?

"Now, as I was saying, are there not Western nations more backward than ours? Are there not Western nations—your own, for instance—where one religion is the State religion? And was not your Anglican faith founded by a monarch who himself had many wives? My father says that Christians and Muslims are cousins, much closer in kind to each other than either is to the Jews. The Jews don't revere Jesus, but we do. My father says as well that your country today is full of gentlemen farmers and gouty politicians who don't know—how did he put it? What a spade is called?

"When to call a spade a spade, that's right, thank you, sir. Your country doesn't understand humility. And yet you are needy people, my father says, and needy people are doomed. Look at the beetle there on my shadow. Simple creature. It doesn't know that it should be afraid. It thinks its shiny carapace will protect it. Your country is like this beetle, sir, a beetle on Allah's shadow. You fancy yourself invulnerable. Not you, I don't mean you. Your people. There is a difference, surely. Just as there's a difference between my brothers and me. My oldest brother, Jamsheed, you know how he would spend his time if he could decide for himself? Making pots and sharing a *huqqa* with other potters. He wanted to ride Anarkali, so I gave him the reins and stood aside and watched. Jamsheed mounted and dug in his heels, but she wouldn't move for him, so he beat her with a stick, and still Anarkali stood there as proud as the most beautiful mare in the Punjab has a right to be, and Jamsheed, he looked like a madman atop a statue. I had a good laugh that day, let me tell you. And I swear my Anarkali laughed too, after Jamsheed had dismounted and skulked away. She flattened her ears, she flicked her tail, and she started to whinny, like this—believe it or not, sir, she was laughing. What do you think of my Anarkali, by the way? You haven't told me. Do you want to ride her? You're not afraid, are you? Have you served your time in the military?

"I ask too many questions, yes, I know, it annoys my mother. Do you have a girl back in England? Maybe you will like my sisters. They're not as particular as Anarkali. It is a funny name for a horse, isn't it? Anarkali. I named her after the concubine of Akbar, who was buried alive because she smiled at a prince. I will take you to see her tomb, if you'd like. And then you will take me to London. Don't tell my mother. She believes what the mullahs say— that all vices come from the West. Not my father—he thinks you people are too stupid to be corrupt. So why are you here? you must be wondering. Why has my father brought an Englishman into his home to teach his son if he has no regard for your institutions? But it's not the institutions he holds in contempt, not your laws or libraries or hospitals or banks. He understands the importance of these in the same way that he understands the importance of a moneylender's gold. You are here to give us your gold, sir. You know, we put cream on our currant buns, we speak your language, we read your books. Yet we haven't grown careless. Look what happens when I flip this beetle onto its back. This is what is happening to you. To your people, I mean. My father says that the West is committing suicide with its own dagger. My mother says that Allah's foot is descending and England will be ground to dust. Like this.

"I hope I see London before there's no London left. Tell me about the taverns, sir, tell me what I should order for my supper. *Cold beef and a pint or two of ale, please.* Is this what I should say? Do I sound like an Englishman? Do you carry a snuffbox? Tell me the truth—do they really tie little girls onto the backs of circus ponies? Does the Lord Mayor eat curried cat's meat for breakfast? Have you ever seen a drowned man floating in the Thames? I don't want to go to London if I can't bring my Anarkali with me. I'll wear a surtout and Bucher boots and I'll ride Anarkali beside the Serpentine Lake—you see, I know more than I pretend to know. I'll have an audience with the Queen, I expect. Will you teach me to play cricket?

"To be frank, sir, I don't entirely share my father's contempt. He has raised me to be one of you, and already I am a stranger to my own family. England is my proper home, though I've never been there. Someday I shall live in London, if the city survives the war. My father wants me to go. He wants me to go and after three years he expects me to return home. But when I go I shall never come back, I know in my heart that I shall never come back. I am as much a foreigner here as you are, and London is my only true home. Please don't tell my father this—if he heard of my intentions, he would take Anarkali away from me.

"You may smile, but without her I would have no reason to live. I know I speak passionately, but that's how it is. Take Anarkali from me, and I will wither and die, just as our fields would if you shut off the headworks of the canals. So now you know why I fear my father. He demands much from all his children, though it's obvious that he prefers me to the others. Still, I have to prove myself worthy. He wants me to study economics, but I would rather be a poet. Maybe you would read my poems and tell me what you think? I compose my poems in my head when I am riding, and I write them down at night, after everyone has gone to sleep. I'm not interested in the science of money: a man who enjoys delicate food doesn't need to train to be a chef, so why should a wealthy man be his own accountant? My father says that after he is gone the bankers will try to take advantage of me. But I am too clever for them. Do you think I am clever?

"My governess—she was Irish, the daughter of a widower who worked as a groom, or who was supposed to work. Mostly he drank beer while his daughter took care of the horses. She taught me to ride. She said I was too handsome to be clever, that boys as beautiful as me are always dull. I don't think she meant it. She was fond of me and liked especially to comb my hair. Violet. That was her name. She taught me everything I know about horses. After she left us she went to live in Amsterdam, and for seven years she sent me packages of black licorice on my birthday. Last year no package arrived, not even a card. I wonder what has become of her. Someday when I'm a famous poet she'll find me in London, and she'll admit that she'd been wrong about handsome boys. She had so many freckles—she let me count them once, seventy-five altogether. She said that's how old she'll live to be: seventy-five. No one could handle horses better than Violet. She broke my arm—did I tell you that? So my father sent her away. Really, he dismissed her because I had grown too old to have a governess, and he didn't think her a proper influence for my younger sisters. She hadn't intended to break my arm. It was a game we used to play. She'd hold me by a wrist and ankle and turn as fast as she could while I flew around her above the ground. One day she lost her grip and dropped me. The bone came through the skin here, you can see the scar. She didn't mean to hurt me. I wonder if she has a husband. The morning she left us I asked her to marry me. Hah, now I consider myself lucky! What if she'd accepted? I would have been obliged to honor my proposal. Maybe you will marry one of my sisters and settle among us. But you Englishmen never settle here. You do your job, you hoard the profit, and as soon as possible you retire to your distant island. I don't mind, though, since I plan to accompany you when you go.

"All this that I tell you is secret, please, at least while we live under my father's roof. But many years from now, when someone asks you to describe your time here, you may report this conversation word for word, as well as you can remember it. You will remember accurately, won't you? Or do all imperialists have an imperialist memory? Will you represent me fairly? Because I think, sir, that in the future someone shall want to hear about me. I am a prince, after all, and you are a prince's tutor."

B's Proposition

There is a tavern, unmarked but not unknown, on the outskirts of Rye. Except for the tile roof rising above the tangle of holly, the tavern, a gray brick structure with stucco molding, can't be seen from the road. B wouldn't know how to give directions to the tavern to someone approaching by car. He prefers to walk there. Usually, he walks alone.

He begins at the railway station, walks across the

tracks, past the jackdaws pecking at the gravel, and follows a raised path leading to a farmhouse. In front of the farmhouse he climbs over a stile and walks up a grassy slope dotted with sheep droppings. At the top of the hill he climbs over another stile. On the other side of Leesam Lane he follows a track that leads past an abandoned farm and the charred frame of a barn to a stream. He crosses the stream and continues through a small clump of trees and along the edges of several fields. Few people traverse this path, so it is up to B to keep the way clear. He carries a hunting knife whenever he walks to the tavern. In early summer the journey takes him two hours instead of one, and his calves burn from nettles for the rest of the day.

At the end of the last field he goes through a gate and hurries past Flint Cottage, always with his hat pulled low over his forehead. He knows the owners, was on one occasion their dinner guest, and made one of his typical social gaffes, something about the hostess's hair, he can't remember exactly what he said but he does remember the glowering eyes of the woman. He hasn't been invited back.

In the meadow behind All Saints Church in Iden Park B rests and takes refreshment. In summer he brings only a pint of strawberries. By the time he reaches the church, the brown paper is stained red, the strawberries inside warm and partly mashed. He lies in the grass, holds a large, misshapen strawberry by its green tuft, and lowers it into his mouth with his eyes closed. He eats all the strawberries this way, one by one, relishing the luxurious surprise as the seeded skin touches his tongue.

After he finishes eating, he dozes for a few minutes in the sun. His large body always feels boyish and light when he wakes, like a feather on the enormous bed of grass. He has read somewhere that, according to the ancients, beyond the Pillars of Hercules the air is full of feathers. How close they were to the truth: beyond the Pillars of Hercules lies America, a continent full of feathers. B, an American by birth but a stranger wherever he goes, is a feather, blown about, from time to time picked up and used to decorate a hat but soon discarded. Though he claims to be an expert seducer, he rarely takes the initiative. Even now, he waits passively for some young boy to come along. What boy wouldn't pick up a handsome feather lying in the grass? B spends most of his life waiting. An expert seducer? As seductive as any ornament—and as useless.

After he leaves Iden Park, B follows the road toward Houghton Green and Appledore, then turns on to the footpath that leads through the holly into the tavern yard. Inside the tavern he sits at a round table covered with green felt and drinks gin. Despite its secluded location, the tavern is never empty—carpenters, lorry drivers, gardeners, and housewives stop in during the day for a pint and a game of dominoes, and the proprietor's children are always chasing one another through the room. On one visit a little red-haired nymph had met B at the door of the tavern. He'd bent down to kiss her on the cheek but she had lifted a cane, tucked the curled handle under her arm, pointed the stick at B, and chortled to imitate a machine gun's rattle before she ran away.

Ordinarily, B stays aloof in the tavern. He enjoys drinking by himself in public places. At social gatherings, conversation dilutes the alcohol, and a man can't appreciate his intoxication. Alone, B can feel the gin taking effect, can enjoy the gradual increase of buoyancy until after an hour his body feels light again, not like a feather on the grass but like a feather floating on the choppy surface of a lake. Floating. B will drink until the midafternoon closing time, and then he'll make the long journey through the fields back to Rye.

"There is a secluded tavern on the outskirts of Rye," B says to K. "I'd like to take you there someday." And K, eucalyptus K, finally frees his hand and draws back with an indignant jerk as though he has burnt his elegant, tender, noble fingers on B's shoulder.

The Challenge

K: "How come you are in such a mess?"
B: "Take me on as a patient and find out."

K: "For my own sake? No thank you, I have little curiosity about others."

B: "You are not going to refuse me?"

K: "First let us see whether we are the sort of persons who can work together."

B: "Then I'd better warn you—I have no unconscious. Now you're going to refuse me."

K: "I am not going to refuse you. Not yet, at least. First I am going to offer you a drink. And then we shall see what we shall see."

Temperature of Equilibrium

K doesn't know yet, not after this first meeting, that B was a prisoner of war in Japan. K doesn't know that in 1936 B left the school where he was studying toward a law degree and went to work in a coal mine for a year. K doesn't know that in B's spare time, when he has no diplomatic obligations and isn't pursuing young boys, he is carrying out experiments on guinea pigs in a makeshift laboratory in his Marylebone flat. His purpose: to accumulate data on animal procreativity. K doesn't suspect that B has any scientific interest whatsoever. But over the next thirty years K will hear at length about B's significant secrets, his past addictions and his latest obsessions, as B continues to live with the same intensity that is so passionate and so destructive.

B will fall in and out of love, will be convicted of pederasty and spend fourteen months in solitary confinement, will lose his job at the embassy and devote himself to scientific research, will publish, and eventually will accept a teaching post at a major American university. He will dream, and K will interpret his dreams. He will confide in K, and K will give him advice, will help B to become more B than B until there is no portion of B's psyche untouched by K. B will become K's arabesque, the patterns delightfully intricate and always symmetrical. B will die without ever regretting K's influence or trying to tamper with the design. B lacks the power, if not the will, to design his own life, and he will give himself up to K. But after his death B will dominate K ("Nothing which has once been formed can perish," Freud wrote), will live on like a parasite, feeding off his host and eventually devouring him. Only after his patient is gone will K admit to himself that from the very first moment of physical contact he was obsessed.

It is the intimacy that makes this initial analytic session more important than any other, forcing K to make a commitment. Yes, he will work with B. He will work upon B. At the end of the session K announces that B does have therapeutic potential, that B might prove to be a valuable patient. They will toast their new relationship.

K pours two drinks, holds his tumbler up to the light,

gently tips the glass so the generous measure of whiskey coats the ice cubes. "Ice," he murmurs. "A luxury." Most Americans take ice for granted, but K, raised in the Punjab, land of fire and water, still considers ice something of a miracle. Ice is water in its purest state, especially ice taken from the tray of K's office freezer. K drinks only the finest Scotch and so insists upon the finest ice made with bottled Alpine water, snow water without traces of chloride, sulfates, nitrates, or ammonia, without traces of human sewage or industrial waste. Pure ice with milky threads at the center of each cube, pure whiskey the color of butterscotch. Luxurious purity. He raises his glass and motions to B, who does the same.

The ice cubes rattle in the glasses. It is important to drink whiskey chilled but not diluted, to finish the drink before the bulk of ice has melted. B drinks with admirable alacrity—not piggishly but with the quick, dainty sips of someone trying both to extend and appreciate a rare pleasure. As B and K drink, from time to time savoring the smell of the liquor, they discuss the artwork in K's office. B learns that the dancer on the pedestal is an original Giacometti. And the cityscape is a Braque. During pauses in the conversation the men swallow in virtual unison, though B, the larger man, takes in more with each sip and finishes before K. He sets his glass on the oak table without thinking about the ring the condensing moisture will leave in the wood. K likes this about B. His nonchalance. B is no aristocrat, but K detects the vestiges of an aristocratic sensibility.

After they have scheduled a second session and agreed upon a fee, after K has escorted B to the lift and returned alone to his office, shutting the door behind him with such force that the polo cap falls to the floor, K feels unusually optimistic, despite himself. Yes, he'd made a mistake in touching B—his hand feels dirty, as though contaminated by B's perversity. He would have to redefine "the correct psychic distance" at their next meeting. But perhaps something had been gained from the brief contact. Perhaps K has established the foundations for a successful transference.

A borderline case. And borderline cases are the most challenging, K knows. How dreadfully easy it is to tip the patient over the edge, especially in the early, blundering phases of the analysis. He must be careful with B, must initially withhold interpretation. Let B do the work. Let B work for him. There is potential here, yes, it's clear to K that there is potential. He stares at B's glass, recalling, without the help of his process notes, B's lengthy narrative, sinks so deeply into reverie that he doesn't hear the six chimes of the Galatea clock and doesn't start preparing himself for the photo session with his fiancée. There is nothing further from his mind right now than his fiancée. He wants to savor this moment. As the nuggets of ice melt into the puddle of lemon-tinted liquid, K's elation grows.

TUMBLING

*P*erhaps I should mention my family's history. There was my father's aunt Martha, who used to chew her lips to bloody shreds; my father's father, who spent the last ten years of his life singing lullabies to his hogs; and my father, of course. He swore to the end that his trouble was just a bum knee and a few quirky nerves. He wore my mother out—she wasn't even forty when we buried her. My brother fled as soon as he was old enough to drive a car, and I haven't heard from him since. So Daddy and I were alone for his last decade. I did what I could for him, all the while dreaming, I confess, about the life I would begin after he was gone. And now I'm like a stone church, steeple intact, standing amid the rubble of a decimated village—my ruin could begin tomorrow.

I was twenty-nine when my father finally died. He left

me a shop full of sheepskins, a two-bedroom house, and the legacy of Huntington's chorea. Give a decent girl two-to-one odds that she is carrying a time-bomb, and even the most desperate romantics will keep their distance. For a long time I waited for declarations of love. None came. So instead I began waiting for fate to reveal its ultimate design. I'm still waiting. These days, with so much time on my hands, I can hardly think of anything else.

At first I was able to support myself selling sheepskins to sympathetic locals. But sympathy was poisoned by hard times, and the cash register drawer stayed closed for so long that I lost the key. I gave up the store in 1977 and moved the sheepskins into the back room of the Skyline Suburban Diner, owned by my mother's sister and her husband. Most days I sat at the Skyline drinking Aunt Josie's watery coffee because I couldn't afford to heat my house.

I don't know what I would have done if I hadn't found a job. Maybe sold my soul, what was left of it. They say every instance of possession by the devil involves a degree of volition. I was that desperate, I would have agreed to almost anything, as long as I wasn't thrown out into the street. If I am to go by way of Huntington's, I want to be able to pull down the blinds and lock the door. It is a terrible thing to witness, and I intend to spare the world the sight.

So when I overheard Aunt Josie and Uncle Jack laughing over a classified ad for an attendant at Riverside Farm, where the sole livestock was laboratory mice, I grew interested. I figured I had a chance at a position that others considered ridiculous. And it turned out to be more ridiculous than I could have imagined: waiting on two thousand mice hand and foot as if they were the fat progeny of aristocrats and I was their nanny. Mice. I'd always hated mice and scorned all the children's stories that celebrated them. Yet still I applied for the job, and the owner, Don MacMurray, agreed to try me out. *Mac*, he called himself. *Mr. Mac* to me. I came to despise him. But at least it was work, my first salaried work, and it is the reason for this story.

*I*n Leatherstocking country north of Cherry Valley, where I've spent my life, there is no level ground, only bluffs overlooking the Mohawk and behind them the blunted foothills of the Adirondacks. There are a few pine groves, but mostly the sloping land is covered with tangled undergrowth and deciduous trees that overnight in October drop all their leaves. One day it is waning summer, the next day the snow begins. Winter lasts until May. But it isn't the persistence that makes winter so offensive—it is the monotony. You can hardly tell the difference between night and day. The sky remains virtually the same flat gray color, the snow is gray, the winter birds are gray: juncos, partridges, hawks. Gray is the color of boredom. Some of us, like my brother Cally, go elsewhere. Some turn bitter. The rest of us are as complacent as the mice. Working, eating, sleeping, fucking, blind to the same dull scenery.

And yet increasingly this is a winter haven for tourists—they drive up from New York City and play in the snow and lose control of their cars on slippery roads at midnight. The few men I dated after my daddy's death were tourists, since the locals wouldn't have me. But even while we banged away in one of the sex-ravaged rooms at the Tiptop Motel, I'd be worrying about the drive home and the steep, twisting decline on Route 20. And I wouldn't relax until I was back in my own bedroom, tucked between the icy sheets and staring out the window at the motes of snow that swirled beneath the streetlight.

I still prefer to sleep alone, with my cat Ellen curled at the foot of my bed. Sleep is full of surprises. I think I must dream in Technicolor. I don't remember my dreams when I wake, but the mood lingers through the morning: a guilty, circumspect satisfaction, like what I felt after I forfeited my job at Riverside. Unburdened, yet vaguely troubled by a whisper of regret.

What you notice first about mice are their eyes. Eyes no bigger than popcorn kernels, sewn into soft pillows of flesh. Gazing out from between the bars of its cage, a white laboratory mouse is able to look both suppliant and accusatory. Multiply one set of eyes by two thousand, and their judgment becomes unbearable—or that's what I felt when Mac led me into the main room. The eyes overwhelmed me, my legs turned to jelly, and I collapsed.

I scrambled to my feet before Mac could bend down to help me. I had nearly ruined my prospects by falling, but I think I landed the job because of my quick recovery. Mac was impressed, I could tell. And he was obviously pleased to see that his plentiful stock had made an impression upon me.

"Wow," I grunted as I picked wood curls off my nylons. Wow. The word tripped too easily off my tongue for lack of anything more descriptive.

"You want *tch-tch-tch*—" In the middle of a sentence it sounded as though his tongue stuck to the roof of his mouth. He gulped and started over. "You want to rest?"

"No, please, let's go on."

"All right, then. These are my *tch-tch-tch*, my, *tch*, my conventionals." Rolling racks lined with cages filled the room, and as Mac led me down a narrow aisle, he tapped on a cage with a long, tapered fingernail, which caused the plump white mice within to retreat into a huddle in the corner.

"Do you have any *tch-tch-tch*—"

"Questions?" I offered.

"Pets!" he cried.

"No, no, I don't have pets. I mean, yes, I have a cat."
As I said it I realized my mistake. Mac's watery red eyes
narrowed, the dark pockets beneath them bunched into
little pillows of wrinkles. *Cat.* It was obviously a dirty
word in this filthy place. Or so I thought. As it turned out,
Mac was more catlike than my Ellen, feral, with a sadistic
appetite for cruel games. I hadn't learned this yet,
though. I thought he was a sweet, lonely man who loved
his mice like children.

He led me into another room, where the air was tangy
with the odor of urine. "*Tch-tch-tch*—" he began. I
wasn't going to risk trying to complete the sentence for
him again, so I waited. "My SPF's," he finally said. The
room was less crowded than the other, the floor was
cleaner. And each cage held a pair of mice identical in
size. "Specific pathogen free," he drawled. "In *tch*—in
time, you'll learn." He clanged on an aluminum water
tank with his knuckles, and we went out to the hall and
into a cloakroom. Mac handed me a hospital smock and a
paper hat and slippers to put on. Then we padded down
the hallway, and at a scratched chrome door he undid the
ring of keys that had been jingling from his belt and
inserted the key into the lock.

I noticed right away that the only odor here was
antiseptic. "These are my GF's," Mac said as he opened
the door. I heard a scuttling within, like glass marbles
rolling down a staircase. "Germ-free. Little beauties."

He inserted his hand into a rubber glove attached to a cage and caught the mouse by the nape of its neck. With his forefinger he stroked it between the ears. The mouse cowered, trembling visibly, squeezing its pink eyes shut as though to will away the caress.

"Darling," Mac crooned. The strange tenor of his affection for the mouse I attributed to the unnatural environment. Each mouse was alone in a sterile isolator, and Mac couldn't touch it directly. I believed that he was fondest of these poor, secluded creatures because he identified with them. I was moved by his eccentric devotion, and I even felt some admiration. He must have been resourceful, I thought. Only mice for company through our long, dismal winters and still completely satisfied.

"They are . . ." I faltered. "They are adorable," I said weakly.

"Aren't they?" The mouse had begun nibbling at the glove, and he encouraged it by rotating his finger until the meaty tip was in front of the mouse's snout. This went on for so long that I grew uncomfortable, and I coughed to remind him of my presence. At the sound his gloved hand jerked up, and the mouse leaped away and slammed into the back of the cage.

"Never cough, do you hear me? Never cough in this room. Never, never cough." He glared at me so viciously that I was frightened—not of him, exactly, but of the potential suggested by his sudden transformation.

Yet after we had shed our scrubs in the cloakroom and were walking down the corridor, he asked me how soon I could start work.

"As soon as you need me."

"*Tch-tch-tch*-tomorrow, then."

I didn't notice that day, but by the end of my first week I realized that in the germ-free chamber Mac's speech was flawless. You wouldn't have known the man had a problem. He never stuttered when he was fondling a GF mouse, never had any trouble expressing himself. *Never, never*, as he barked at me that first day without stumbling over a syllable.

Which is where I'd come to work: a scientific never-never land, where anything was possible, as long as someone could think of it.

With a full-time job, I no longer spent hours at the Skyline. But Aunt Josie and Uncle Jack let me keep my sheepskins there, and one day at the end of April my aunt called me at work to tell me I had a prospective customer. At first I thought it was an insulting joke, and I almost hung up. But right then a man's voice came on the line and introduced himself as Burk. He'd been admiring my sheepskins, he said, and went on to describe their qualities with words like "resilient," "plush," "velvety," all lies and each adjective enunciated with the crisp precision of his German accent. Yet I admit I felt flattered, as though he'd been speaking about me. He said he was interested in purchasing six of my skins. Six! I tried to sound brisk, businesslike when I replied. I agreed to meet him after work. "Then we'll see," I said. But as soon as I had replaced the phone in its cradle, I let out a shriek of joy.

The phone was in Mac's office. Fortunately, he'd stepped out for a minute. When he walked back in he asked me what my aunt had wanted that was so "*tch-tch-tch* damn important" she had to call me at work. I said, "Nothing," and bounced into the corridor, savoring the luxurious daydream of money.

But a strange, chilling recognition, a sort of déjà vu, came over me later while I was walking along Route 39. I thought about my first customer in years, this foreigner named Burk, and pictured his face. I felt that I remembered him. The memory was inspired by no more than his voice during a brief phone conversation, but I felt even before I saw him that his arrival in the region was a return, that he had passed through long ago, that he was one of the most acceptable men I'd ever seen, and that again, as before, I would be captivated. And yet I believed—no, I was *certain* that we'd never met; recognition was no more than a wish spun from the paltriest incentives.

Call it clairvoyance, but I was right about the attraction: my customer had the sleek, high-cheekboned profile of the spoiled rich, and yet there was a softness about him, too, as though his face were made of wax. Light brown hair tumbled in curls to his shoulders; his lips were so deeply red that I thought they must be glossed; his torso was concave like a runner's; his rump was narrow, tucked neatly between his hips. And though he must have been close to forty, he looked an unaging twenty-five.

Face-to-face, the sense of familiarity became even more insistent without shaking my conviction that I'd never seen this man before, nor had I set eyes on his friend, a dark, bulky, southerner named Oscar, about ten years Burk's junior. At a glance I could tell that there was no room for me between them. I think I sagged visibly as Burk extended his hand to me, and Oscar slipped from the booth and stood beside him. And to add to the humiliation, Aunt Josie and Uncle Jack smirked in the background, as though they had intuited the nature of my disappointment.

I was wrong, as well, to doubt Burk. The sheepskins smelled musty. Many were discolored on the underside with a violet mold. But Burk had already selected the skins he wanted, and he offered me five hundred dollars for the lot of them, a fair price, I thought. Even better than fair. As I watched him carry away the hides, his purpose became clear to me: he intended to fill those skins with blood and flesh and bring them back to life. It was an absurd idea, of course, a childish fantasy, but for a moment it made complete and reassuring sense.

I learned from my aunt that the "Kraut," as she called Burk, and his friend had purchased a costly parcel of land on a cliff overlooking a wide bend of the river and were building the weekend house of their dreams. When they came up from the city, they stayed in a Winnebago parked in their driveway and drove around in an old Chevy pickup, playing at country life as though they were in a TV sitcom—which only made the locals resent them more. All tourists are considered parasites, but the worst are the ones who pretend to belong. And when the Kraut's friends started to flock into our enclave and to buy up our land and to peck one another on the lips in public, our men turned livid. I waited for the rage to explode into violence. I knew that as soon as the last construction worker had put the finishing touches on the house, the bounty hunters would go to work.

I had bought a '67 Mustang with Burk's five hundred dollars, so I was able to drive where I pleased. Every weekend I concocted chance meetings. I hung out at the Skyline all morning until Burk and Oscar came in, tousled and swollen from too much sleep, for a late breakfast. I shopped for groceries when they usually shopped—midafternoon on Saturdays. I drove past their Winnebago a dozen times a day. And whenever Burk saw me he would nod, his red lips would part in his luscious and slightly sarcastic smile as though he thought me reckless, and I'd smile back, then turn away so he wouldn't see my tears. For I'd become as weepy as an adolescent again. I cried myself to sleep at night. I cried as I cranked the bottle-rack turner at work, I blathered and wept, and then wept harder when I looked in the mirror and saw what the tears had done to my face.

But that was only stage one of my infatuation. In the next stage I said, *Girl, pull yourself together*, and I decided that I'd take it upon myself to protect these strangers from my murderous neighbors. There would be no lynching. No explosion. No vandalism. I would put myself between the fag-bashing mob and their intended victims. It would be much more noble, this sacrifice, than the lonely dwindling I'd expected for myself.

But the months passed, and the simmering hostility boiled away to nothing, pure, innocent nothing. The custom-designed dream house, a three-tier A-frame, took over a year to build, and in that time the locals grew numb from a recession that wouldn't give up. A mild winter unfolded into drought; the drought lasted through the next winter; the snow came late; the tourists didn't come at all. Except for Burk and Oscar and their friends—they were reliable year-round, and most of the locals came to appreciate them for this.

So the Kraut didn't need my protection. That second winter he rode around in the passenger seat of the red pickup, Oscar at the wheel, both of them wearing tall sheepskin hats with the woolly flaps pulled over their ears. Burk was a fashion designer and had sewn the hats himself, I learned from my aunt, who used to banter with the two men as she poured their coffee. But by the middle of winter they no longer showed up at the Skyline. They were too busy entertaining. Their driveway was always jammed with cars, and at night the woods around the house echoed with the jazz from their stereo. I would park down the road and open the window and listen until the cold air burned my throat. Their parties lasted all night.

I hardly saw them anymore, except on the road passing in their pickup at fifty miles per hour, and then I could only catch a glimpse of Burk's face beneath his hat. The last time I saw him up close he and Oscar came into the 7-Eleven to buy a newspaper. I had just paid for a quart of milk, and I pretended to fumble with my change. I noticed that on Burk's cheeks were two circles of red from the wind, like the chapped patches on kids who have been sucking Popsicles too long, and the rest of his skin, in contrast, was a pale plastic.

At first I thought he hadn't seen me, but as he brushed past to the door, he said, "They're a hit among my friends," pointing at his sheepskin hat. And this time his expression had a twist of malice to it, not aimed at me but including me, conspiratorial, I thought. For a brief, delicious moment, we were all alone in the world.

*T*he winter stretched on, cold and overcast. Snow eddied in continual flurries but only dusted the earth. I spent most of my time feeding mice and cleaning their cages and packaging them to be shipped to research laboratories around the country. The conventionals were on a liberal diet, and since Mac cut costs whenever possible, we supplemented their food with items picked out of Mac's garbage. I grew so used to the smell that I wasn't aware of it after the first five minutes of the working day. The SPF's and GF's were monitored more closely and ate only sterilized feed. In the afternoon, I changed their bedding and washed and replenished their bottles. And when the germ-free mice were being "derived," as it was called, I stood between Mac and the Professor (I never knew him by any other name), who came once a week to perform the operation. Mac handed the Professor surgical instruments, and I took them from him when he was through.

To derive germ-free mice, you need to preserve the newborns in an uncontaminated state. What was involved was this: first Mac selected a pregnant mouse from the conventionals, broke its neck, then shaved the abdomen and soaked the carcass in a sterilizing solution and pinned it to a cloth. At this point the Professor took over. He covered the abdomen with an adhesive plastic drape. He made an incision through the drape and skin. He snipped the ovary ligaments and removed the fat uterus and placed it in an air-blown plastic isolator. Working from outside the isolator through rubber gloves, he cut the uterus open and removed the tiny pink pups one by one.

The Professor was as nondescript as a winter day. Mac was the one whose eyes glittered with pleasure as he cracked the necks of the mother mice. The only part I enjoyed was watching the Professor free the pups from their sacs. But I paid close attention from start to finish and memorized the details of the elaborate operation so completely that I could have performed it myself.

All the skills I was acquiring at Riverside Farm, however, would be of no benefit to me, I knew. There was no future in the mouse business. My heart wasn't in it. My heart was in one place, and that place had no future.

I slept through the fire that gutted the dream house one night in late February. We all slept through it, even the volunteer firemen on call. The fire must have burned for hours before old Mrs. Jelliman, an insomniac and always the first to notice anything out of sorts, smelled smoke a half-mile away. It was the middle of the week, and Burk and Oscar were in the city.

By the time the single firetruck arrived, nothing was left but the foundation. The iron gate had been warped by the heat and leaned open onto the brick walk. The aluminum sides of the Winnebago were crusted with soot, and it sat in the driveway like a dazed witness. The firemen smoked cigarettes as they idly sprayed the earth with water to contain the remnant flames. All they could do, or all they cared to do, was to keep the fire from spreading into the woods.

It was Aunt Josie, as usual, who related the news to me the next day. She'd learned about the fire by eavesdropping on a conversation that morning between some local boys—Twain Gierson, his brother Hal, and the meanest thug of all, Chuck Fen. They had laughed and flicked matches across the booth and tried to outdo one another with descriptions of the fucking awesome flames and smoke so thick they almost suffocated. Of course, no one would ever accuse them of arson. Even though the locals had forgotten their feud with the strangers, they still had a responsibility to their own kind.

That night I parked my car on the road in front of the ruins and rolled down the window. The air was still acrid with wet ashes. Out of habit, I found myself listening for some sign of life, the beat of percussion, singing, laughter. But not even the woods made any noise that night, though the wind was strong enough to set the branches and treetops in motion. I had the impression that the trees were swaying to music that I couldn't hear. And if I couldn't hear the music, then I wouldn't be able to hear the cadences of voices mingling in the yard, the crash as champagne glasses were flung against brick. The party hadn't ended. Burk and Oscar had come back to celebrate, and the Winnebago shook from the vibrations like the body of a giggling child. Yet I had no more awareness of the celebration than I ever had of my dreams. I felt as though I were awake and dreaming—experiencing the dream without imagining it. The only thing I could imagine was Burk's face beneath his sheepskin hat, his cheeks burnished from the wind. It made me shudder to think of him. I rolled up the window and locked the door, and eventually I fell asleep to the clamor.

I woke to someone tapping on my windshield. It was Don MacMurray and his tapered fingernails. He'd been driving to the early-morning service at his church and had recognized my car. It was an odd sensation, looking out at his shadowy form through the frost-crusted glass.

Was I tch-tch-tch—*okay?* I told him my car had stalled and turned the ignition to demonstrate. Miraculously, the engine revved and caught. I thanked him for his concern and drove away.

*M*onday morning at work he didn't even mention the incident. He was too distracted to think of it. Apparently, one of the labs we supplied with mice reported that their latest shipment of GF's were suffering from the early stages of Tyzzo's disease, a form of hepatitis. Before I'd arrived Mac had already found dozens of conventionals dead in their cages. All the SPF's and GF's were alive, but a few seemed more humpbacked and languid than usual, Mac thought.

When the Professor appeared at noon, it was decided that two of the GF's must be sacrificed. In both autopsies, the livers showed "traces of necrotic tissue," as the Professor put it. And just as dryly he advised Mac to slaughter his entire stock of GF's and SPF's and to quarantine the conventionals. They couldn't risk sending out infected mice. The bacteria must have been introduced into the sterile environment, the Professor said, through the food or water or bedding. Then he glanced at his watch. "Leave a message with my secretary to let me know when you need my services again," he told Mac, putting on his coat. "Good day to you both."

I, of course, had been responsible for the food and the water and the bedding, so I expected to be Mac's scapegoat. We stood in the corridor, watching the Professor let himself out the front door. As soon as he had gone, I turned to face my employer, expecting the worst. "Mr. Mac," I began, intending to apologize. But instead of accusing me of sabotaging the feed or spiking the water, instead of threatening to deduct the cost of my treachery from my paycheck, Mac took a few steps backward, as though gently pushed, stumbled over his feet, balanced himself, and pulled from the deep pocket of his lab coat a listless mouse, probably about three weeks old judging from its size. He stroked it for a moment. And then, while I watched, he made a fist around the mouse and squeezed. I heard—or perhaps imagined—a slight popping sound. The crevices between Mac's fingers filled with blood.

With a smile, Mac told me to stop standing there like an idiot and get to work. I went straight to the broom closet. He watched me sweep for a while, sneering, I assumed, at my compliance, and then with a grunt he took away the bloody trophy in his hand and left me to my work. When I heard the door to his office shut, I said under my breath, "Pig." And again: "Pig." I pushed the pile of dirt against the wall. "Pig, pig, pig, pig, pig." And for the first time in my life, I contemplated revenge.

I've been doing some reading. One of the experiments our mice were used for, I've learned, is known as drum trauma and is designed to test for the effects of battering. An unanesthetized mouse is placed inside a motorized metal drum, its paws taped together. The drum revolves forty times per minute. A standard trial consists of three hundred and sixty revolutions in nine minutes, and the mouse falls seven hundred and twenty times. The typical injuries sustained are: teeth knocked out, internal hemorrhage, engorgement of the bowels, kidneys, lungs, and intestines, shock, and eventually death. The scientists call it "tumbling."

Another experiment used to explore pain tolerance is

electrical stimulation. The mice are anesthetized for surgery, and electrodes are implanted in the pain receptors in the brain. When the animal wakes from the general anesthesia, the electrodes are stimulated for sixty seconds. An experimental session consists of twenty to sixty one-minute trials. Sometimes, as a cost-saving measure, instead of being anesthetized for the surgery, the mice are injected with the drug curare, which paralyzes them without reducing the sensation of pain.

One of the strangest experiments I've read about is *parabiosis*: under anesthesia, two mice are surgically joined side by side with metal skin clips, and the inner linings of their abdomens are sewn together. Some mice live for months in this condition, but most die as a result of "twisting," when one mouse in the pair turns itself on its back while the other mouse remains right side up.

But let me describe the one experiment of my own design:

Mac chose to delay his pleasure and scheduled the slaughter for Tuesday morning. "We'll do it together," he said, patting my shoulder—the first time he'd ever touched me. "Just the two of us."

I stayed late on Monday evening, telling Mac I wanted to finish cleaning the dip tanks. He didn't argue. After he left, I propped open the front door to the building and I built a barricade with empty trash cans at the opposite end of the main corridor. I unlocked the door to the GF chamber, and one by one I peeled off the sterile plastic covers, lifted out the mice, and put them on the floor.

Never having been outside their isolators, they thrust their snouts into the air and sniffed, their whiskers trembling, and hardly moved from where I'd set them. Once I'd freed them all, I nudged them gently with my broom toward the door. They slid along the linoleum like pairs of rolled white socks, then all at once hurry-scurried in a pack out the door and down the hall.

Next I freed the SPF's, all two hundred of them, and drove them out of the room and watched them scuttle dizzily toward the open air. And then I returned to the conventionals. Their cages had removable bottoms, and I simply slid the racks out and the mice dropped with the snow of wood shavings to the floor. There were over a thousand, too many to gather into herds. So I scattered feed along the front walk to lure them outside, and I left them to discover freedom for themselves.

By the time I went home that night, the linoleum floor was slippery from the pee of excited mice, and everywhere you looked you'd see them cleaning their whiskers, resting on their haunches, mounting one another, and even, I thought, laughing at my madness.

I spent the evening dusting the many odds and ends that I've collected from yard sales over the years—old Coca-Cola bottles, ceramic salt and pepper shakers, a stuffed parakeet, a hobbyhorse, mock-Tiffany lamps, china tea-cups. The night passed, and there was no knock on the door. The phone didn't even ring. I sat at home through the next day and the next, petting Ellen, watching televi-sion, drinking bouillon to soothe the symptoms of a cold I'd developed. A week passed and no one came after me. Finally I ventured out, as timorous as a germ-free mouse. I bought groceries, and Barb at the cash register asked casually how I'd been. *Pretty well*, I managed to say. I bought medicine at the CVS. I bought a newspaper. Everyone knew me in these stores, but no one seemed to suspect what I'd done.

My last stop was the Skyline. Uncle Jack came out from the kitchen and poured me coffee. Josie, he said, had gone home at noon with the flu. The diner was empty—the supper crowd hadn't arrived yet. Uncle Jack asked me to give him a hand that night. I'd waitressed for him before when Josie had been sick, and though I myself was miserably congested, I put on a black lap apron trimmed with white frills and began clearing dishes from a booth. I stopped to sneeze violently, and when I had recovered my uncle asked me how things were going up at Mac's place. I didn't know what to say. He asked again, and I told him I'd had enough of mice and had quit.

"Speaking of mice," he said, aiming a pair of spaghetti tongs at the wall. They clattered harmlessly to the floor. "Goddamn mice," he seethed through overlapping front teeth. "And listen here, you get those filthy hides out of my diner, or I'll be condemned."

I didn't have to go into the back room to know what I'd find: my two thousand plump wards nesting happily in my sheepskins. In fact, when I turned on the light I caught only a glimpse of white hindquarters slipping through a hole in the baseboard. But there was evidence: crumbs and wood dust on the floor, tiny black pellets sprinkled in the wool.

It took two weeks before a delivery driver discovered the empty cages at the farm. Apparently, Mac had left town to escape his creditors and angry researchers—for years he'd been folding one loan on top of another. People assumed he'd been the one who had freed the mice, and they cursed him for their troubles. Sometimes I joined them by shaking an angry fist at the mention of his name. Exterminators came flocking. Tourists and locals alike invested in poisons, but the mice grew as bold as flies and more cunning over time. The ones with Tyzzo's died off, the healthy ones reproduced. They were known to jump up on a kitchen table and steal a bite of hamburger from a child's plate while the mother's back was turned. For the most part, though, they were invisible and indulged in their crimes in skilled secrecy.

The first victims of the mouse epidemic have been the cats. Her nocturnal hunting so exhausts my Ellen that she can hardly drag herself to her food and doesn't even bother with the litter pan. My neighbors will be the next to succumb. Everyone is in debt, jobless or fearing for a job. People see the mice as the emblem of their poverty. Kill the mice, they tell themselves, and life will improve. But so far the mice have triumphed.

And to think I'm to blame. For a while my secret complicity made me feel superhuman, as worthy of legend as the Pied Piper, if I ever dared to confess what I'd done. I didn't bother looking for another job right away. My cold persisted and gave me an excuse to coddle myself. In the afternoons I took to wandering around the land behind the ruins of the dream house. Oscar and Burk hadn't returned since the fire—they'd put the land, along with the Winnebago, up for sale.

One sunny spring day I climbed onto the trailer's back bumper and wiped a circle clear in the grimy window and peered inside. The interior was still furnished, still looked inhabited, for that matter. Still *was* inhabited. Beyond the bunks and the Formica slab of a table, I saw two white mice hunched on the counter and one sitting in a frying pan on the portable stove, clutching a crumpled piece of foil between its paws.

Mice. The entire community had been taken over by mice. And I was the insane culprit who had freed them in the first place. I must have been out of my mind, I thought. And just then, as though to assure me that I really had gone mad, the air filled with a rolling thunder punctuated by loud clashes, similar to the sound of a highway collision. Shorter blasts followed the first. The sound couldn't have come from the clear sky, nor from the interstate, which was ten miles away. I climbed down from the trailer and headed toward the explosions, or into them, as though I were walking into the sun. I walked toward the river, right to the muddy edge of the bluff.

In Rip Van Winkle's day rumbling in the mountains was made by bowling balls and pins. I looked down at the river. The *boom boom boom* echoed from an inlet, and I understood at once what it signified. The ice was breaking up. Oddly, in all my thirty-eight years, I had never heard this sound before. But who knows? Maybe every winter the river greets spring with this tremendous thunder, and I just hadn't noticed.

It was an unreal noise, entirely echo it seemed, as though it had no origin. I searched the vaporous air for an image of the sound and grew dizzy. I felt as if I were falling and with every boom hitting a hard surface—like a body tumbling inside a revolving drum. The rumbling echoed behind my ribs as huge blocks of ice tore apart and collided. I stood there and imagined tumbling, tumbling, seven hundred and twenty times every nine minutes, unable to save myself from the next fall, unable to stop the drum from turning.

But it meant nothing. After all the ice had been sucked

downriver and the pounding had stopped, I was just the same as before, unbruised, no broken bones, still passably rational. The river was quiet again, unnaturally so after the clamor of the spring thaw. Everything alive waited for the next great change, and I waited along with it, caught in a state of nearly unbearable suspense.